DEUS VULT

ST. TOMMY, NYPD BOOK SIX

DECLAN FINN

SILVER EMPIRE

Dedicated to all those who fight the good fight, no matter what.
Because God wills it.

1 / VISITATION

My name is Detective Tommy Nolan, and I am a Saint.

More importantly, I am father to two beautiful daughters and a son who becomes more colorful by the day.

I held one of them in my arms. My two-month-old daughter, Grace Gabrielle Nolan, squirmed and laughed in my embrace, nuzzling me, trying to bury herself deeper in my body.

I sat back on the front porch swing and held her close. I was strangely content.

Perhaps it wasn't that strange. The front porch was to a New England summer house owned by our local Medical Examiner, Doctor Sinead Holland. It had a few acres of land, and the edge of the property line wasn't a fence, but a treeline. While it wasn't summer, it was still early spring. The air was crisp but pleasant.

"She's a cuddler," my wife, Mariel, stated as she sat next to me. Mariel had long, wavy chestnut brown hair, round, deep-brown eyes, a pleasant heart-shaped face, and a healthy olive complexion. She wore a red and white floral cotton midi dress that set off her figure very nicely. Her Espadrille wedges were her pride and joy, giving height without sacrificing comfort. But she could wear a burlap sack and I'd still want to keep making babies with her.

She also looked out at the kids playing in the yard. Though "playing" was a strange word for it. My son Jeremy threw things up into the air, while our newly-adopted daughter, Lena, proceeded to hit them with objects that she tossed with her mind.

Yes. Lena tossed them *with her mind*. A telekinetic teenager wasn't the strangest thing that I had ever come across in my life—or even the last two years—and it was less supernatural and more science fiction. Only without the fiction. A friendly neighborhood theologian (yes, there are such beings) says such things are called preternatural, not supernatural.

"Pull!" Lena called, her thick Polish accent making it sound like *pool*.

Jeremy threw a fistful of grapes into the air. A box of toothpicks to Lena's right sprang to life as a collection of them darted out like shotgun flechette, each grape speared by a single toothpick.

Then, as much as to show off as to not waste food, Lena plucked each grape out of the air (with her mind) and piled them on a plate on her left.

Mariel laughed at the display. "She's fitting in well."

I smiled at her, then at Grace. "It helps that we have a flexible definition of 'normal.'" I leaned down to touch the tip of my nose to Grace's. "Don't we, Gracie?" I asked her.

Grace giggled. I touched my forehead to hers. "Headbutt of love."

Mariel wrapped an arm around me and leaned into me.

It was idyllic.

The front door opened, and my partner, Alex Packard, stepped out onto the front porch. He wore khakis and a matching polo shirt. He covered a yawn as he looked out at the children playing. He ran his hand over what little hair he had left. "Well, Tommy, I have to hand it to you. You know how to collect colorful characters."

I ignored my partner. Sardonic, sarcastic, and cynical were his default positions.

Mariel lightly nudged him with her foot. "Oh, leave off, Alex. You like her, too."

Alex shrugged casually. "Sure. She's a nice kid. And she hasn't made my brain explode. Which is even better."

Mariel sighed, dismissing Alex's comment. I said nothing as I focused on the bundle of joy in my arms. Grace was such a strangely perfect little baby. I didn't remember Jeremy being anything like that when he was born. He had been eager to get out of the womb and came out swinging, his little fists latching on or touching something— usually as fast as possible.

Besides, if I replied to Alex's comment, I might have to mention that when I had first found Lena, it had been only a few feet from what was left of the men who kidnapped her. They had each been horribly murdered. Lena had done it with her mind. Though to say that they didn't have it coming would be a lie. But spreading that around would have only served to make people touchy around her. Just a guess on my part.

But in the two months since I had brought Lena home from Europe, she blended in like we had raised her from birth.

Jeremy and Lena ran up to the house. Jeremy wore a black sweat-suit. Lena wore a frilly pink dress that we could barely get her out of ever since we bought it—she'd seen it in the store, fell in love with it immediately, and would have slept in it if we didn't suggest that it might be ruined. She beamed as she ran after my son, showing how pretty she really was.

Jeremy ran up with the plate held up in front of him. "Look what Lena did!" he boasted on her behalf.

I nodded. "I saw. Very nicely done. Really good aim."

Lena beamed. She even bounced a little.

Alex smiled sardonically. "Hey, Jeremy, I thought you didn't like girls."

Jeremy looked at Alex like he took offense. "Lena's not a *girl*," he said in her defense. "She's *awesome*."

I smiled at them both. "Come on guys, let's go inside. I'm cooking omelets."

The children cheered. Alex smiled sleepily. Mariel kissed me on the cheek before she got up to join them.

Jeremy stopped, pivoted to face me, and asked, "Daddy, what's Mary like?"

I stopped halfway to standing up. I frowned and furrowed my brow. "Um ... personally? Why do you think I would know?"

"Well, who visited you before you got your superpowers?"

I paused, confused, cuddling Grace close to me. "I met John Paul II last month. Does that count?"

Jeremy frowned, confused. "In stories, I've read, someone shows up *before* you get the charisms. So who talked to you?"

"Sorry ... no one did."

Jeremy blinked. "Huh." He shrugged, and we went inside.

Doctor Sinead Holland was already up and setting the kitchen table. *I guess I'm predictable*, I thought. I had spent the last few days getting up, walking to church for 6 a.m. mass, and coming home to find the house alive, awake, and ready for food.

Sinead smiled at me. She was a pretty brunette with brown eyes that always caught the light. Her background was Northern European, up near Norway, giving her high cheekbones and eyes that were nearly Asiatic. She wore a green and red madras cotton shirt (a few years old) and some loose faded jeans, plus a straw sunhat with wide green band. Her shoes were Israeli army issue, which are sturdy enough for farm work and go with any outfit. She managed to look polished despite "dressing country." Her words, not mine.

"Good walk this morning, Tommy?" she asked knowingly.

"It was good," I said, as always.

I hadn't actually *told* anyone I spent my mornings at church. Everyone figured it out already, but everyone had allowed me to not discuss it.

It wasn't that I was embarrassed to go to church, but I didn't want to talk about my visits to church. My relationship with God had become both simple and complex at the same time. He had granted me charisms in abundance—powers and abilities that came directly from God, and only manifested by Saints. I had a box in the trunk of my car directly powered by God. The ring on my finger was a mystic rock that had real-world effects to heal humans and hurt demons—it might as well have been the Ark of the Covenant.

Everyone else thought it was obvious that I would be a canonized a saint. While I've stopped trying to talk them out of it, I didn't have another explanation. While I wasn't complaining that my son thought I was a superhero, or that I had been able to defeat the forces of darkness multiple times via the grace of God Himself, my constant question was, *Why me?*

The only answer I kept getting was, *Why not?*

As I cooked breakfast on the stovetop, operating four fry pans at a time, Alex entertained the kids with yet another magic trick. He kept giving me vague hints that it had saved his life at least once while I was away, but we hadn't gotten around to discussing that yet.

Alex held up an ace of spades. "This one really isn't a magic trick. This is an ordinary playing card. Nothing special about it. Touch it, feel it, don't bend it out of shape, though. The edges aren't modified in any way, shape or form."

Once Lena and Jeremy finished examining the card, they offered it to Sinead. The good doctor smiled, raised her hands, and shook her head. "Thanks, but I've seen this trick."

Jeremy shrugged and handed it back to Alex. Jeremy leaned back against Lena, and she leaned into him.

Alex placed a grapefruit at the center of the table and leaned back in his chair to create a little more distance. He lined up the grapefruit with the card and snapped his wrist forward. The card sliced into the grapefruit, driving half of the card into the fruit.

Alex brought the chair down with a thump. "It's literally all in the wrist!"

Lena laughed and clapped. "I want to do it!"

Lena looked at the pack of playing cards on the table. The top card shot off the deck and sliced into the grapefruit at one end and halfway out the other.

Ten other cards shot out one after another, turning the grapefruit into a pincushion of playing cards.

Alex looked from the grapefruit to Lena. "Show-off."

Lena merely smiled at him. She and Jeremy shared a high five.

I said nothing and kept cooking.

Then the doorbell rang.

I turned the heat down low on all the burners with my left hand and grabbed my gun with my right. Alex was already out of the chair and grabbing his gun. It was before nine in the morning, so it wasn't the mail. And this was a summer home. It was rare for anyone to be here. If we were lucky, it was someone looking for an empty house to rob or squat in. If not...

Alex looked at Sinead. "Does anyone know you're at home?"

She shook her head. "Only my husband, and he's not due in for a few days."

Alex and I moved to the door. He braced himself to the side, and I had my hand on the handle. I was torn between checking the peephole and just opening the door so we could get the drop on whoever was on the other side.

This wasn't paranoia. This was Tuesday.

"Detective Nolan," came a British accent through the door. "I would appreciate it if you didn't shoot me."

The stress left my body but entered my soul. It was one part of my world I hoped would never again come near my daily life and threaten my family.

I opened the door, and there stood Father Michael Pearson, a terribly average-looking priest. He was of medium height, with a sturdy build. The build was deceptive since I had seen him in hand-to-hand combat. Pearson wore typical black-on-black-on-black for his pants, shirt, and jacket. He was bald, mid-forties, with a closely-cropped brown beard. His eyes were brown and warm and friendly, hidden behind glasses with black frames so thick they looked like they had been borrowed from Clark Kent.

Except Pearson was my partner when I worked missions for the Vatican. I only saw him when something world-destroying needed to be stopped or when the fate of millions hung over a pit.

Pearson smiled at me. "Detective Nolan, you're needed."

I walked Father Michael Pearson into the dining room and introduced him. "He's my partner abroad."

Packard smiled and offered Pearson his hand. "I'm the partner local. He get you in any trouble?"

Pearson gave a flicker of a smile. "I'm afraid I'm the one who brings trouble to him."

Lena charged in and threw herself at Pearson, hugging him around the waist.

I looked at Packard and said, "They've met."

Packard arched a brow. "Obviously."

I introduced Pearson to the rest of my family and friends. He was good-natured and polite to everyone. They continued to chat as I finished cooking.

"So," Mariel said in a tone I could only call suspicious, "how did you qualify to be Tommy's partner?"

"I have a certain set of skills."

Jeremy said, "You don't look like Liam Neeson."

Pearson smiled and waggled his brows. "Different set of skills."

I came out with three plates and handed them out to Mariel,

Jeremy, and Lena first. "You want to explain what you're doing out of your jurisdiction?"

Pearson smiled and shrugged. "My jurisdiction is God's."

"You know what he means," Mariel said darkly.

Pearson blinked, taken aback at her tone. "I'm sorry, did I say something –"

Mariel leaned over the table. "My husband keeps collecting scars," she growled. "From injuries that would have killed him had he not been six places at once. You think I like it that you're anywhere *near* my husband *or* my children?"

I had a sudden tingling in my palms, where I had two of the scars she mentioned. I had enough new scars from my London trip to look like I had a recurring case of stigmata, including one in each foot and my side. I was close to collecting a whole set. This didn't even count the scars left behind from a Rikers Island riot where prison bars had been torn off and speared through me like a butterfly being pinned to a wall.

To say that Mariel was less than thrilled with new scars was to put it mildly.

Pearson blinked, confused. "I'm sorry, I was under the impression that you were supportive of your husband's –"

"I am!" she snapped. She leaned over the table so far, I worried her hair would get in her breakfast. "I just want him to have a partner that *also* supports him. I've seen no evidence that you're good for anything but bringing him trouble and plenty that you're good at getting him into it. Now what. Do. You. Want?"

Mariel leaned back and dug into her omelet, stabbing it while staring daggers into Pearson. She'd rather be stabbing Pearson.

Alex leaned over, and stage-whispered, "Yeah, Tommy, I don't think Mariel likes Pearson."

This was putting it mildly. Mariel was sweet and kind and loving. She would casually have a shotgun at the dinner table, but she would be friendly and pleasant throughout dinner until the zombies showed up at the front door. That happened.

This Mariel? I hadn't seen her this upset since a Deputy Mayor insisted that I would be thrown in jail for throwing the last Mayor into Hell.

Okay, he was dragged, but let's not be picky.

Pearson nodded slowly. I left the table to retrieve more plates. He kept talking as long as he saw me through the opening between the kitchen and dining room.

"There is a nearby Passionist monastery. I presume that you're familiar with them?"

I came out with plates for Sinead, Alex, and me. I sat and shrugged. "Catholic religious. They focus on the Passion, obviously. They preach missions and retreats. They teach people how to pray. Sometimes, they assist local churches. They don't open schools and universities, except seminaries for bringing people into their institution."

Pearson nodded. "And they have many members that are exorcists."

Alex cringed, thinking about our first demon. "Aw crap," he muttered. "Not again."

I dug into my plate. I had sauteed the onions and the mushrooms on different pans, then threw them in with the hash. It worked nicely. "Okay, so what's the problem at the local Passionists? Did they lose someone in the course of an exorcism?"

Pearson took a deep breath and slowly let it out. "Not exactly. They lost...everyone. The entire monastery. Early reports state that the exorcists were murdered first. Then the rest of the monastery was slaughtered. The entire building has been desecrated to Hell and Back."

Alex frowned. "Literally, I'm sure."

Pearson sighed. "And these are just the early reports. We've gotten as much input as we can from the boots on the ground, but there is only so much that a local priest can get away with at a crime scene. There's only so much the local Bishop will authorize, or risk."

Sinead frowned. "That doesn't sound like something that the Pope would tolerate."

Pearson smiled. "Pius XIII? He's not tolerating it. That's why I'm here. And since Tommy is also here, the mission—should you choose to accept it—

"Does he have a choice?" Alex interjected.

"—is to investigate and find out exactly what happened there."

I frowned, thinking over what Pearson just said. It didn't make any sense. If this was a local crime, shouldn't we have heard of it? "When did this happen?" I asked.

Pearson's lips tightened, unhappy about the events. "Yesterday morning."

Mariel still sounded suspicious as she asked, "How come we haven't heard about this in the local news?"

Pearson smiled. "Remember when some nutcase shot up a mosque in New Zealand, killed a few dozen, and no one would shut up about it for days?"

Mariel nodded. "Of course. It was more like weeks. Why?"

"How much did you hear about the churches bombed in Sri Lanka for Easter 2019?"

Mariel sighed. "If I hadn't heard about it from the pulpit, I wouldn't have heard about it."

"Exactly." It was Pearson's turn to be unhappy and growl. "*That* slaughter killed over two hundred people, and if you didn't get your news from a real world newspaper, you probably didn't hear about it. Even then, it depended on the newspaper."

I looked around the table at my friends and family, then tapped my plate. "Can I at least finish breakfast?" I asked.

Pearson nodded. "Take your time. It's not like the crime scene is going anywhere. The bodies have been carted away, but everything else is intact."

Alex coughed, chewed some more, and swallowed. "Since I'm the only one who's legally allowed to carry, you're not going without me."

Sinead sighed. "I should tag along as well. You're not going to have any local forensics except for me. So I might as well."

I looked at Sinead and nodded. "Okay, but you're going to take your own car. You look at the crime scene, give us your thoughts, and when you're done, you come straight back here. I don't want anyone out in the field any longer than necessary. That includes me, but I, at least, have a gun..."

Mariel gave me an amused look. "You forgot the basement."

I didn't laugh, but she was right. Mariel had brought our collection of guns with her from the house in New York to the safe house in Tennessee. Then she bought more to add to the collection. It's the primary reason that we drove up to Massachusetts instead of flying.

"I don't think we should carry those around the city *just* yet. Besides, we both know I have a few tricks up my sleeve."

Both Mariel and Pearson looked at the ring on my right hand. To all appearances, it looked like a college ring, with a similarly large jewel in the center. Though in this case, the jewel looked like a multi-faceted rose cut diamond, set in a black and silver band. Like a college ring, it had two emblems, one on either side of the jewel. One side was the Crusader Cross of Jerusalem—a cross with four other crosses, one in each quarter of the primary cross. The other emblem was a shield, like a family crest, in front of the crossed keys and papal crown of the Vatican flag. The shield looked like it had an inverted sword on it, forming a cross—the coat of arms for the Swiss Guards. The shield displayed the coat of arms for the current Pope.

The only difference between this and a college ring is that it held part of the Soul Stone.

The Soul Stone had been a prehistoric artifact that had nearly left London a smoldering hole in the ground. It had been around before Abraham, before polytheism, when monotheism was a natural, instinctive idea. It had been given to the people of First Dynasty Egypt by ... something big, scary, and powerful that would later be misinterpreted as Anubis. The jewel had not been cut off of the Soul Stone, but *willed* off, by someone with excellent concentration.

Right now, my faith, my prayers and God powered the Soul Ring.

That didn't even count the *really* interesting armor in the trunk of my car.

Lena looked at me. "Hussar, are you going to ride to the rescue again?"

I smiled at her, and her name for me. She insisted on calling me the cavalry. "Let's hope not."

We finished breakfast ten minutes later. I rose from the table, cleared every empty plate, and made certain to kiss Grace on the forehead before I got my overcoat. I kissed and hugged Lena and Jeremy. I told them to listen to Mariel and say their prayers.

I made certain those were the last words they heard from me on the way out the door ... just in case I never came back.

3 / WALKING THE GRID

As we got in the car, Alex said to Father Pearson, "Tell me again how we're going to get into the crime scene?"

"The police are finished with it, so they don't care if we look around or not."

We pulled up to the crime scene a little after ten AM.

The local Passionist monastery was medieval and pleasant. It looked a little like a castle, only with windows made for air circulation instead of arrows. Looking on the website, the frames had been home to beautiful stained glass windows.

I had to check the website because every last stained glass window had been smashed out.

The windows smashed, the crosses ripped off the walls and smashed with a hammer...the outside only hinted at the desecration within. Before I stepped out of the car, I smelled the evil within. It reeked worse than any crime scene I had ever been to. It was often like that with the scent of evil.

Within the monastery was the worst crime scene I had ever witnessed. Ignore that every religious image had been torn, smashed and stepped on, and *then* smeared in blood or excrement or both. Ignore that every piece of furniture had been overturned and ripped apart. Ignore the images of Christ ripped off each crucifix and ripped limb from limb.

Ignore all of that, and it was still a nightmare from a blood-spattered horror film.

According to the file that Pearson had received from the local police, the Passionist monks had all been stripped naked and dismembered to various degrees. Ten of them had been disemboweled. Five of those had been strung up from the rafters for their guts to hang out of their bodies. Some had been left in poses that were less suggestive and more flat-out pornographic statements. Every monk had had their genitals removed and reinserted elsewhere.

Even without the bodies, it was horrific. It was nearly impossible to differentiate between the smell of urine, excrement, blood, vomit, and evil.

Alex led the walkthrough, and I wandered behind him. When circled the area, nodding slowly and cataloging the damage. "Let me see if I got everything. Bloody finger paint on the walls. Desecrated bodies. Desecrated crucifixes. The altar has been burned and struck with hammers. The pews have been torched. The tabernacle has been blasted with a shotgun. Bodily fluids left on the marble—it looks like someone had sex there, but it was only semen in one aisle and only female fluids in another. It's like the set design for a horror movie if someone used a wood chipper and a full morgue."

I held up a hand to stop him. My stomach had finally had enough. "Okay, I have to step out."

Alex followed me outside. I went straight for the car... then kept walking across the street. I wanted to run but restrained myself until I could no longer smell the death, decay, and filth from the crime scene. I couldn't bear it any longer. My tolerance was decreasing over time instead of getting better. As the smell of sin and evil was metaphysical, I couldn't block it out with something as simple as cotton balls dipped in alcohol to make the smell go away. I couldn't wear a gas mask. I couldn't –

Wait. I don't have a gas mask, but I do have a faceplate.

I turned back and went straight for my car's trunk. Alex ambled out of the monastery and sauntered over. He was used to coming after me when the stench became too much.

But he wasn't prepared for this.

I opened the trunk, and there was a steamer trunk inside. I flipped the locks, and opened it up. Inside was a suit of armor, only it was made of clay. It looked like parts could belong to a terracotta Iron Man. But I only wanted one part—the helmet. It looked like it could have been a Tony Stark invention, only the face place was blank, giving it an appearance more like a fencing mask. I had decided I didn't want it to stand out with the telltale markings of a Templar suit of armor. Blank and anonymous were more my speed if I had to wear it in public.

Let's see if this works.

I slid on the helmet, and the face mask swung down of its own accord, sealing into positing.

Filter the air, I thought at the armor.

I could suddenly breath clean air.

Instead of a black void in front of me, the world became brighter and more vivid.

Then again, that's what happened when one's vision was enhanced by the Divine Spark.

The armor set was created from the remains of several golems, made and created by a Rabbi of Prague. The golems had been smashed by demons, but that didn't matter. No one had thrown the off switch on the clay automaton. And what God had brought to life, let no demon rend asunder. The pieces and parts of golems had reformed around me as a suit of powered armor. And since the golems had no eyes, just the shallow place for them one might see like the eyes of a department store mannequin, their way of seeing was more akin to sensors or scanning equipment... Holy Radar, if you will.

In this case, the golem transferred the sensor data to an augmented reality screen before my eyes.

"What's with the helmet, Darth Vader?"

I smiled beneath the mask. "I need something to help me breathe."

Alex looked me up and down. "I don't see any air holes in that thing. How are you breathing *now*?"

I patted him on the shoulder and waved him back to the monastery. "I'll explain on the way."

We walked back inside, and I filled him in the trip to Germany. He shook his head. "So you have a magic ring and a magic helmet. When do you get a magic spear and start singing opera?"

"Hopefully never."

I stepped into the monastery again and paused. Suddenly dots of blood were clearly visible. Clear fluid stains were highlighted with colored outlines.

The golem helmet runs on power from God. It can see everything.

I thought at the helmet and had it filter out only the smell of evil. After that, I checked off one thing at a time. Urine. Fecal matter. Blood.

Then I caught something. The smell of burned paper.

I waved at Alex to follow me as I tracked the scent. It led me down a hall, around a cluster of chalk outlines, (it wasn't really chalk, just markers for reference points) and into the main office of the monastery's abbot. I looked around the room, trying to find the source of the burned smell. All of the papers were off the shelves and all over the room. Papers carpeted the floor and everything in it, even the overturned office desk. The only void in the papers was where the bodies had been.

I pointed to the center of the room, where I smelled the burning. "Help me clean this off. Watch the papers, they may have missed something they wanted to burn."

After five minutes of going through every sheet of paper, we had dug down to the overturned desk. Packard and I exchanged a look. That the desk had been left in place did not speak to the efficacy of the Essex police department. We shouldn't have been the ones to dig through the papers. If the papers had been left in place, that meant that the crime scene had been released to us without sorting and cataloging every piece of paper. It also meant that no one had gone through the abbot's desk. If I did that at any point in my career, I'd have been fired. Even my first day on the job as a detective, I would have been obsessive over the details, making sure I cataloged everything—it would have also made the evidence room hate me since I would have cataloged items that probably weren't even evidence.

Alex placed the last piece of paper on the pile. "You know, I don't think I ever screwed up a crime scene this bad, even when I was drunk off my ass."

I dropped to a crouch and focused on the desk. "No blood, so they didn't bother," I told him absently. "Just a guess."

"Dumb asses," he muttered. "Let's get the desk upright."

Alex and I sufficiently gloved up before we grabbed and righted the desk.

As I figured from the smell, a small pile of ash sat underneath the overturned desk. I dropped down to my haunches and spread the ashes with my finger. The augmented vision of my helmet highlighted three pieces of paper that escaped the fire. The edges looked like they had been torn apart, then burned.

Should have burned it straight, then sifted through it, I thought.

I took the three pieces and fit them together. It was the name of a company, Matchett Industrial. "Well, that doesn't help."

"What doesn't?" Alex asked.

I tapped the pieces. "Matchett Industrial? Ever heard of it?"

Alex frowned, thought a moment, and shrugged. "No. Sorry. I've heard of Matchett *Investments*. That one is your basic hedge fund. Is it something?"

I shrugged, holding the pieces together so I could place it on the desk behind me. "No idea. We'll see."

Pearson stepped in the room. He carried what looked like the remains of a sign-in book. It was clearly burned as well. He looked at me wearing the helmet and said nothing about it. "Hello there. Find anything?"

I gave another glance around the office to make sure there was nothing more. "Very little. Why? You?"

Pearson placed the book down on the desk. He flipped it open and slid out five different sheets of paper. "These are all from yesterday. Sign-ins for different times. Different names. And they all signed in a company ... though don't ask me which, there are more holes in it than I know what do to with. Something with a lot of Ts."

Alex and I exchange a look.

Alex smiled. "Well, Pat, I do not want to buy a vowel, but I would like to complete the puzzle. How about Matchett Industries?"

Pearson looked at him, furrowed his brow, then looked down. He shrugged. "I guess. How did you figure that?"

"I'm really good at crosswords," Alex answered.

I turned to face Pearson squarely. Before I said anything, the helmet highlighted a rectangular object stuck to the side of the desk. It was the same color as the desk, which is why we hadn't seen it earlier.

Probably why the killers didn't notice it either.

"But you know what this means, right?" Pearson asked. I turned my attention back to him.

Sinead tapped the door as she stepped in. "What does what mean?" She looked to me. "And *what* is that on your head?"

I waved her off. "Later."

Pearson tapped the sheets. "The sign-in register. This means that there were *multiple* people here for *multiple* exorcisms."

Sinead nodded and opened the files with the crime scene photos and held them up as they became relevant. "That fits with what I found. There are least six different weapon types I've found, and ten different hand sizes—figure six men, four women. This is the low number. That probably means that there were at least ten killers."

Alex held up his hand. "Hold on. No. Hell no. I am *not* doing this crap again. You're telling me that we have *another* situation like Curran, but more of them?"

I inwardly cringed but kept my face placid. I happened to be in agreement with Alex. Christopher Curran had been a serial killer. There had been dozens of victims to his name. They had all been buried in his basement, in pieces. That was *before* Curran had been possessed by a demon raised by a death cult. When possessed, he was nigh unstoppable. He had hurled cars with his mind, ever so casually. He was arrested after I had filled his joints full of bullets. Later, it seemed that he had *wanted* to be caught as part of a grander plan. What finally defeated him had been a combination of trickery and brute force prayer.

I shook my head. "This time, we know what we're doing," I told Alex. "If we knew then what we know now, we'd call in the right backup as part of our confrontation. We have Pearson. We only need to get this right *once*."

Pearson cleared his throat and raised a finger. "For the record, I feel I must clear up a misapprehension. The typical exorcism isn't anything like what you see in a movie."

Sinead frowned. "I thought the book for *The Exorcist* was based on a real-life incident."

Pearson shrugged. "That case was a more dramatic instance. Demons in possession cases *rarely* manifest that blatantly. Most cases of demonic possession want to be low-key. The moment the demon is discovered is the moment things go south for it. It's why it would sooner manifest as depression, or crippling disease, or a host of other symptoms. It's why the first job of any exorcist is to find a doctor who will both acknowledge demonic possession is a possibility, and will first rule out every other possibility. It's not *that* big a problem these days, since the exorcists I know only get a knock on the door *after* every doctor in existence has written the patient off."

Alex sighed and held up both hands, signaling a pause. "Okay. Hold up. I didn't read the book, but I saw the movie. If that's not SOP for an exorcism, what is?"

Pearson shrugged. "It's more of a process, and the Rite itself is literally only ten percent of the job. Ninety percent of the work must be done on the part of the possessed—be it from a routine of prayer to daily mass and regular confession. It can take *years* of blessings to fully rid the possessed of a demon. It's more of a treatment than a cure. And all the while, the demon is fighting back... in many cases, the demon is trying to convince the victim that there is no demon. Demons don't exist. Obviously, the victim is just crazy."

Sinead took a deep breath and slowly let it out. She wasn't happy. "Anything else?"

"There can be a relapse. Because if you're not penitent, it's going to screw things up a bit. As in there's very little that can be done if the possessed *wants* their demon."

Alex sighed. "Great. Where does this lead us?"

I looked back to the rectangle on the desk. I reached down and slowly peeled it off. It was a business card. "How about to a Mister Gerald Downey, of Matchett Industries?"

THE FOUR OF US CONTINUED TO SCOUR THE REST OF THE
monastery but found nothing. After, Alex, Pearson, and I went to
Gerald Downey's house, while Sinead got in her car, wished us luck,
and drove back to the house.

"Can't I go with her?" Alex asked as she drove off.

"Come on."

"At least take the helmet off when driving, okay?"

It didn't take long to find the home address of the Gerald
Downey who happened to work at Matchett Industries. We looked
up Gerald Downey, found five different individuals, and then picked
the one that lived nearest to the company. Then we drove to the
house.

How did we know that we had the right Gerald Downey? I
opened my car door and the smell of evil knocked me back on my
heels.

Pearson and Alex both noted me—it was hard not to, I grabbed
the hood of the car and doubled over, trying not to vomit.

"How bad?" Alex asked immediately.

"Curran smelled better."

With his left hand, Alex reached into his back pocket and came out with a box for playing cards. With his right hand, he reached behind him and adjusted his gun.

Pearson shifted his own weight, touching three pockets in his jacket, checking to see what was there. "Will you be all right?"

I hesitated. I didn't want to say *yes* flat outright. If I didn't get used to this, I was going to be in serious trouble. There would be no way that we could avoid a confrontation. If Downey was possessed (and with the state of his house, there was no way he wasn't at least dabbling in the demonic) then his reaction to me would be much like Curran's ... he would try to kill me, instinctively and immediately.

I looked at Pearson. "Break out your holy water. I think I have a solution."

I walked around Pearson and popped the trunk. In the wheel well, we had a first aid kit. I grabbed a cotton ball and tore it in half. I rolled each half into a tight ball, then waved Pearson closer for his holy water. I tapped the holy water onto each ball, then tapped them into my nostrils.

I took a deep breath.

The scent of sin was gone.

"Whew." I reached up, grabbed the trunk, and slammed it shut. I looked at Pearson. "I wish I had thought of this a year ago. It would have saved me a lot of bother." To Alex I said, "Let's go."

We approached the door cautiously. Pearson still held the vial of holy water. Alex had a firm grip on the playing card box. I had a little plastic pouch of holy oil in my left hand.

When we knocked on the door, a teenager answered. Her age was hard to gauge, since she deliberately dressed down, but she looked *painfully* young. Her brown hair was in pigtails, and the baby fat in her face made her looked prepubescent... except, she was pregnant. She was otherwise tiny in every direction.

"Can I help you?" she asked in a high soprano voice.

I reached into my pocket and flashed my badge. My left hand still had the holy water. "Yes, my name is Detective Thomas Nolan. I'm with the police. And who are you?"

She leaned back, the door half-closed, like a shield. "Denise."

I nodded and slipped my badge away. "We would like to talk with Gerald Downey. Is he in?"

"He's not here right now," she told us.

I glanced back at the others. They shrugged. I smiled at her genially. "May we come in and wait for him?"

Her body language went stiff in a particular way. I had sudden flashbacks to every domestic disturbance call I had ever rolled out to. Which, unfortunately, led me to wonder who the father of her child was.

"Don't worry," I said, "we only need to ask him some questions." *For the moment.*

Her eyes narrowed. "About?"

I shrugged casually. "We know he had visited a monastery yesterday. We would like to know if he can help us with our inquiries. Maybe he saw something. Perhaps he even did something we need to know about." *Like murder a bunch of helpless exorcists.*

"I guess." She stepped back and took the door with her. I smiled again, nodded, and stepped inside. I didn't want to spook her with sudden movements. She closed the door and asked if we wanted coffee. I thought she'd feel comfortable if she were in with the knives and we were in the living room.

I nodded. "Sure."

She left. Alex and I exchanged a look. I nodded at him. He nodded back. Pearson watched us. He said nothing but moved with his back to the wall.

"If she didn't live here, I'd consider torching the place and see if that sent a message to the bastard," Alex said under his breath.

I said nothing, but I had similar violent thoughts.

There is one call every cop hates—domestics. They were volatile, unpredictable, and there were few ways to really tell who was the victim and who was the perp. That's even assuming every party wasn't both to some degree. Though in this case, I was willing to place money on who was the perp and who wasn't. I almost hoped that Gerald Downey was guilty of being some sort of otherworldly and supernatural creature. That would give me an excuse to pummel him into the dirt.

He causes me to lie down in green pastures; He leads me beside still waters. He restores my soul; He leads me in paths of righteousness for His name's sake. He prevents me from taking a tire iron to Gerald Downey's skull...

My friends and family wondered why I doubted being a "saint." Because I knew exactly what went on in my head.

Denise came back and offered coffee all around.

"So, when's the happy date?" I asked as I took the cup.

Denise looked at me, confused. She distributed the rest of the coffee. I nodded towards her baby bump.

She flinched. "There won't be one." She gave a brief glance to Father Pearson. "I'm going to have an abortion," she said sadly.

Pearson was deliberately looking the other way. Alex focused on the front door.

Okay, fine then. "Aren't you a little far along for that?" I asked casually as I sipped the coffee. "I'm thinking you're at least five months? Perhaps six?"

"Oh, my stepfather says that we can go down to New York City at any time before she ... it comes. We hear that Mayor Hoynes made certain it could happen up to the last minute... before he disappeared."

Before he was dragged to Hell, you mean, I thought. Alex smirked. I could see he thought the same thing.

I looked around, then looked at her. "If you're going to wait that long, might as well consider adoption. Talk to anyone about that? I mean, you seem in good shape. Good living environment. Your daughter would be a shoe-in for almost any home." I reached into my badge holder and slid out my card. "Give me a call. All else fails, I'll adopt her. My wife will be happy that she's not giving birth to this one," I joked.

Denise snatched the card and slid it away.

A car door slammed outside. Denise's head shot up like a startled gopher. I placed the coffee down. "Denise. I think you'll want to go upstairs now."

Denise didn't have to be told twice. She moved as fast as she could up the stairs. A moment later, we heard another door slam, her bedroom door.

I placed myself in front of the door, standing fifteen feet away. I wanted to be the focus of Downey's attention when he first came in. Alex took up a position in a corner of the room at right angles to me. Alex could flank Downey when he came in. Pearson stood diagonally from the door. All we needed was Downey to complete the square.

The door swung open, and Gerald Downey took a step inside before coming to a dead stop.

Downey was not a tall man, but he was stocky. His hair was graying, so was his mustache. His eyes were a pale sickly blue, hidden behind wire specs. He had big rough hands that seemed disproportionate to his size.

Downey smiled broadly when he saw me. His teeth were so oversized, they looked fake.

"It had to be you, didn't it... Saint?"

5 / HELL SPAWN

THE BOOKCASE BEHIND ALEX LEAPED OFF OF THE WALL, dropping on him. It spilled books and DVDs all over him and the floor. He cried out in the surprise at the sudden attack by the inanimate object.

From the wall, the plasma television dropped onto Pearson. It was a light television, but it still slammed into his back with enough force to throw him to the floor.

The couch swung around, coming for my legs.

O LORD, oppose those who oppose me. Fight those who fight against me.

I jumped in place, my feet coming down on the couch cushions. It didn't matter, because the couch jerked back, ripping my feet out from under me and throwing me to the floor. I tucked my chin and slapped the ground with my forearms so I could absorb the impact on the fleshy parts of my body and not the bone.

Put on your armor, and take up your shield. Prepare for battle, and come to my aid.

This left Downey free to jump for me. From a standing start, he cleared the length of the living room to body-slam me.

I planted my left foot on the floor, shot my hips up, and launched my free foot in a kick, planting the sole of my shot in Downey's face.

Lift up your spear and javelin against those who pursue me.

I planted my right hand on the floor, pushed up, and swung my right leg under me. It shot back and shoved to my feet.

Let me hear you say, "I will give you victory!"

Downey and I now squared off, his advantage against me gone. Downey was low, his back hunched over, gorilla-like. His arms were wide, ready to reach out and clasp me if I got too close.

I clenched both fists and smiled. "Not so easy, am I? You don't fight me. You fight the Lord."

Downey grinned, excited. His breath came in quick, shallow huffs. "Good. I would hate it if this were too easy."

Downey charged.

Bring shame and disgrace on those trying to kill me—

I shot my hips backwards and my left hand to palm him in the face. For the record, in any other situation, that is a truly dangerous move, and would be as like to break the defender's fingers as anything else.

However, in this case, my fist had burst the bag of holy oil, covering my hand and fingers in it. The oil covered Downey's face in a mask he couldn't easily wipe off. My fingers drove into his eyes. The oil on my palm went up his nose and on his lips. He roared and reared back like a horse that had stepped on a caltrop. The windows rattled, and my eardrums hurt. He swatted my arm away and swung for my head. I leaned back, letting the blow fly past, then burst forward so I could ram the scar on my palm into his nose. With a *crack*, his head snapped back, and he staggered towards the front door.

Turn them back and humiliate those who want to harm me.

A lamp ripped out of the wall and flew for me. I dropped to a crouch. It smashed into the wall, covering me with shards.

Downey growled. "How dare you! You think you can defeat me! Defeat us! If you only knew the true *power* of—"

Alex, from his place on the floor, had drawn his gun and fired. Downey's kneecap exploded. He cried out in pain, the leg collapsing. He wheeled around to Alex. This only served to present his face to Father Pearson's uppercut. Downey rocked back, slammed up against the wall. He hissed like a snake and pushed off the wall. He launched his shoulder into Pearson's body, sending him back across the room. On one leg, Downey whirled on Alex. My partner fired again, but the demon hopped, dodging the bullet.

"Aw crap," Alex muttered.

Blow them away like chaff in the wind— a wind sent by the angel of the Lord.

I jumped on Downey's back, overbalancing him. We went crashing to the floor. Downey snapped his elbow for my face but only caught my bicep. The impact made my entire arm go numb. I slammed my oiled palm into the side of his face and pressed his head into the floor. Downey cried out in pain and thrashed beneath me. He bucked and tossed me something fierce and eventually threw me off.

Make their path dark and slippery, with the angel of the Lord pursuing them.

Downey rolled over, coming straight for me. His fingernails had grown during our fight, looking more like raptor talons. His teeth took on a more ratlike appearance. He gnashed his teeth at my face. I pulled back just in time. His claws shot in as my arms came out in a guard. The talons slashed my overcoat to ribbons and caught my flesh as well. My blood quickly covered my arms. He darted forward like a snake, his teeth coming for my neck.

Let sudden ruin come upon them!

Instead, Downey's teeth met Pearson's shoe as he went for a full soccer kick to the face. Downey fell back and went rolling away. He pushed himself off the floor, onto his good leg. His features became more snake-like. His eyes were slitted, his tongue flicked out and back again.

Let them be caught in the trap they set for me!

Downey looked at Pearson. "And who are you, little priest? Should we know you?"

Pearson shrugged. His hands were clenched in fists. "Perhaps. I've faced any number of you fools."

Downey's grin expanded. "Fools? We know all that there is to be known. There is nothing in existence that we do not know. We have existed before your foolish faith, and no matter what you do to me today, we will exist long after you're gone."

Pearson smiled. "But I'll be in Heaven. We know where you'll go." He spread his arms wide. "Come. Let's hug it out, as the Americans say."

Downey hissed and threw himself forward.

Pearson spun, opening his right fist, throwing holy salt in Downey's face, as well as twisting out of the way of Downey's charge.

Let them be destroyed in the pit they dug for me.

Downey ran into the holy salt and roared. His momentum carried him forward into the wall.

Then I will rejoice in the Lord.

That's when I pushed off my feet and body-checked him, driving him further into the wall.

I will be glad because he rescues me.

He shoved off the wall, throwing me with him. He whirled, slashing at me. He scored across my chest.

From the floor, Alex had gotten his box of cards and slid one out of the pack. Except it wasn't actually a playing card, but a metal card with a saint's face on it.

He reared back, and like with the regular playing card and the grapefruit, he flicked it into Downey's face.

The metal card bit into his cheek. He hissed and shook it off like a bear with a bee sting.

However, Downey's strength left him. His face morphed back to the features he entered the house with, and he fell back. He collapsed to the floor like a switch had just turned him off.

With every bone in my body I will praise him: LORD, who can compare with you? Who else rescues the helpless from the strong?

Pearson and I scrambled forward to secure Downey. I flipped him on his stomach and cuffed his arms behind his back at the elbows —when I had faced Curran, he had dislocated his thumbs to get out of handcuffs. I wasn't going to risk that this possessed bastard would do the same.

I kicked the door closed, then sagged on Downey's back. I didn't care if I was too heavy for him. It wasn't like I was going to kill him.

I let out a heavy breath as the tension drained out of me. I found myself suddenly out of breath, gasping for great gulps of air.

I rolled over on my side and looked to Alex. "You okay?"

Alex gave me an acid look as he pulled himself from under the bookcase. "Just peachy, Tommy." He grunted as he pulled himself forward. "You know. I am getting *way* too old for fistfights with demons and witches and whatever else is hunting you."

I blinked, confused. I thought over all of my experiences with Alex. "What witches? And when did you start carrying metal holy cards?"

Alex reached forward again, then went limp. "Screw it." He sighed and planted his face in the rug. "Long story. I'll tell you about it sometime."

THE THREE OF US TOOK GERALD DOWNEY AND DRAGGED HIM UP the stairs. Pearson and I had a grip on his shoulders, Alex on his good foot. Alex let the damaged leg *thump* against every step on the way up. Downey woke up screaming at the first *thump* and kept screaming all the way up. We couldn't tell if the demon had woken up and was play-acting, or if it retreated into Downey and hid from us.

I looked over my shoulder at Alex and said, "Really? You had to do that?"

Alex smiled and shrugged. "Kinda."

I rolled my eyes and kept hefting as Downey swore a blue streak all the way. After a while, I tuned out his threats of lawsuits, damnation, and physical violence. Back in my uniform days, that was a Friday. We tossed him into the first open bedroom door. It was the master bedroom...

Conveniently, the master bedroom had a four-poster bed and physical restraints already attached. It was almost like he knew we were coming.

Yes, I'm making light of the situation. My current state forbids me from dwelling too long on what my thoughts were at that moment.

My first reaction was quickly quelled. I didn't know the situation between him and his stepdaughter (thank God, rape was bad enough without incest on top of it) for certain. I didn't want to assume *too* much. Downey, pre-demon, could have just been into some kinky bondage stuff. Which, according to my faith, it perfectly fine as long as Tab A ended in Slot B where it belonged. Contrary to popular belief, the Vatican largely didn't care what happened behind closed doors, as long as it was consensual, between a married couple, and everyone was fully open to conception.

I threw Downey on the bed and didn't care when Alex took the injured leg and "accidentally" slammed it against one of the bedposts.

Without being told, Pearson moved to the other side of the bed to secure Downey's arms with the provided restraints.

Alex chuckled. "Not your first rodeo, huh?"

Pearson looked at Alex and shrugged. "My title is combat exorcist. This is an easy day in comparison. They're usually shooting at me."

Alex scoffed, amused. "Funny, me, too."

When Downey was as fully restrained as we could make him, I said, "I'm going to check on Denise. You two going to be good here for a few minutes?"

Alex shrugged. "I got commando priest here. What could happen?"

Pearson rolled his eyes and waved me on.

I could tell they were either going to be great friends or kill each other. It was a coin toss.

I stepped out into the hall and went to the only closed door. I knocked on it. I made certain to frame my next statement in the full knowledge that she had heard the gunshots downstairs, and part of the fracas. Since she was a minor (I think), and I was a cop, I turned on the voice recorder app on my cell phone before I knocked.

"Denise? This is Detective Nolan. All clear out here."

I heard a few clicks of a lock. Denise cracked the door to make certain it was me. She opened it a little wider to see behind me.

When she saw I was alone, she threw open the door and hugged me. She broke down into tears and deeply saddened me with tales of her abuse over the past three years—psychological, emotional, physical, sexual, the whole gamut of major and minor meanness. The confession of suffering and grief she had been put through just came pouring out.

I stood there and took it, returning the hug and saying nothing. When she said, "He wanted to wait to kill my baby when she was ready to be born. He wanted her cut to pieces when she was still alive." I made certain not to show my anger. She didn't need anger at that point.

I didn't time how long we were there like that, but it was a good chunk of time. She needed to tell someone about everything, and I wasn't going to stop her.

"—and then all of this weird shit kept happening after he ripped open the walls and put them back together again. Things kept moving when my back was turned. There's always banging in the house when I'm alone. And I swear the shadows keep moving."

My blood turned cold, and my body tensed. I looked around and felt the sudden urge to get Denise out of the house while we still could.

Not a bad idea. "Denise, do you have a neighbor's house you could go to? We're going to have to talk to your dad for a while. You may not want to be around for that?"

Denise smiled. "Are you going to torture him?"

I smiled at her in understanding. "Not quite. No."

Her smiled fell. "Oh. Okay. Sure. I can get somewhere."

I nodded. "Before that, can you tell me where some of the sealed-off walls are?"

ONCE DENISE WAS SAFELY OFF AND RUNNING, I WENT BACK TO the master bedroom. Pearson busily prayed over Gerald Downey.

Downey constantly snapped at Pearson with his teeth. Pearson backhanded him once without even breaking stride in the Rite.

Combat exorcists, able to multitask. I waved to get Alex's attention, and he came out, closing the door behind him.

"Geez, Tommy, where the heck have you been? I've been in crack houses that were less scary than that room."

"Don't worry. I got something just as scary."

Alex sighed. "Of course you do. I—" He cut himself off as he looked at the wall next to him. I had drawn a big X in the wall with a folding knife I carry. "Was this here when we carried *The Omen* in there up the stairs?"

I shook my head. "It's in the walls."

Alex looked at me like I had lost my mind. *He should know better by now.* "Is that an *Amityville Horror* quote?"

I arched a brow at him. "The only horror I know of in Amityville is a convent of Dominican nuns that live out on Long Island. Come on, we have work to do. First, we have to find a hammer."

Alex rolled his eyes. "Here we go again."

We spent the better part of an hour breaking walls in Downey's house. We found sticks wrapped in ribbons, nails, little ivory dolls no bigger than my little finger, ribbons wrapped in bows, hair wrapped in string, etc. We ended up with a Xerox box full of miscellaneous crap. We took it outside, and Alex pulled out a package of red dust and poured it on the hoodoo.

He smiled at me and said, "Thermite," before dropping a lit match on it.

The thermite burns at twenty-five hundred degrees. It's enough to burn a hole through a car's hood, and the engine block beneath it.

This pile burned for a minute. It set the surrounding grass on fire.

When the thermite burned away, the hoodoo pile was unscathed.

We both stared at the pile and blinked at it. I looked to Alex and said, "Should I even ask why you carry that on vacation?"

Alex gave me side-eye. "For the same reason I carry metal saint cards. You're back in town. I carry this stuff like I would carry my badge and gun. There's a reason I kept my suitcase in my back seat. My trunk is so full of thermite, I better not get rear-ended. I might burn a hole in the highway." He nodded to the pile. "The real question is what we do with this garbage if it doesn't want to burn?"

I looked at the pile, blessed it with the sign of the cross, and even pulled out another packet of holy oil. I sprinkled all of it on the pile of ribbons and sticks and ivory, said another blessing just to be sure, and looked to Alex. "One more time."

Alex nodded and pulled out another pack of thermite. This time, it all burned.

Between Denise's crying, the demonic Easter egg hunt throughout the house, and breaking most of the walls and floorboards, we had killed the better part of three hours. I pulled the cotton balls out of my nose to sniff the air. It was clean.

"We're good to go. I think Downey's been purified."

We made it into the house, and found Father Pearson coming down from upstairs.

"So, von Sydow," Alex started, "how did everything go with Downey?"

Pearson smiled weakly. He brushed past us to head for the couch. He fell into the couch and sagged, exhausted. "He's clear of possession. I made him say the name of Jesus Christ." He bowed his head at The Name. "Usually, it's not something they can do when possessed."

Alex frowned and walked over to an armchair across from Pearson. "You *made* him say it? Or you had him say it?"

Pearson arched his brows. "Oh, I made him say it. Part of what makes a combat exorcist different from the usual routine is that we deal with hostile hosts who *need* to be exorcised but don't want to be. People like your Mister Curran. Or Mister Downey. It's more of a brute force approach. The effects would almost certainly be considered cruel and unusual punishment. Injections with holy water, liberal use of holy oil and salt. He's practically wearing a collection of saint cards. And I had to punch him a few times when he got out of line."

Alex arched a brow. "That doesn't sound that bad."

Pearson scoffed at Alex's casual statement. "Oh, really? I'm essentially driving out a parasite from the man's soul. You ever see what happens when you brute force a leech? It isn't pretty. There's risk for psychological damage *on top of* whatever self-inflicted spiritual damage he's done to himself. There's a reason there aren't many people who are up for this job. Now, do you want more of my CV, or would you like to know what I learned?"

I cocked my head, surprised. "He actually talked to you?"

Pearson waved the question away. "He was out of it and didn't really know what he was saying or who he was saying it to. From what little I figured out from my conversations with Downey—and I should specify it was not the demon, but *Downey*—we are definitely dealing with several other possessed.

Alex groaned. "No flipping way." He reached into his pocket, pulled out a cigarette and lit up. "How in the he—"

Pearson held up his hand to cut off Alex's next complaint. "It *must* be deliberate. There's no way that this many demons came to possess this many people in the same place and time without something deliberately orchestrating it."

I raised my hand. The scar that looked like a railroad spike had driven through it always caught the attention of the room. "But they came to the monastery. *Several* people came to the monastery. The sign-in sheet *said* they were there for exorcisms. You figure they did it to themselves and had second thoughts?"

Pearson nodded as he reached forward for his cold coffee. "Somebody did." He took a sip, then paused. "Okay, at least *one* person did. Perhaps he or she ratted out the others. The possessed generally have to come to the church to have anything happen. Or family refers them to an exorcist."

Alex laughed. "Quick! To the diocese, Batman!"

Pearson and I looked at Alex. "Why are you laughing?" I asked.

He blinked. "I thought I was being funny. Why? Are we actually going to talk to the Bishop?"

I nodded. "We'll have to. But first things first."

It took another hour to talk to the local police so Downey could be dragged away for attempted murder of a Church investigator (technically, me) and a cop (Alex), and a priest. Alex spun the narrative and naturally left out all the details of demons and possession.

Denise's mother would be home to pick up *those* pieces. I left my card behind with my cell phone number, just in case she wanted help reassembling the living room. And perhaps plastering the walls.

I was not surprised that I never got a call back.

7 / CARDINAL TAPE

IT WAS THREE-THIRTY IN THE AFTERNOON BY THE TIME WE GOT to the diocesan office. It was difficult enough to update the cops on everything we had to tell them. It was even more difficult to get an appointment with the Bishop. It took forty-five minutes of aggressive driving to go from Downey's home on the outskirts of Boston to the city center.

The archdiocese of Boston took up all of eastern Massachusetts. If you wanted to see a Bishop, you talked to Boston, pure and simple. It was annoying since we had several Bishops and even a Cardinal for New York City alone, and Massachusetts had one diocese for nearly a third of the state—and based in the most corrupt city *in* the state. There was a Cardinal Archbishop, who was away doing his duty for the Catholic Development Fund and not available for comment.

The diocese was housed in the Cathedral of the Holy Cross. It was the largest Roman Catholic church in New England. When it was built in 1875, it was designed to rival the local Protestant churches—a not-so-subtle dig at those who had treated the Catholics like dirt.

Like every Catholic neighborhood, you can usually find them in areas people look down on. For example, the cathedral is located in the city's South End—or "Southie." At the time, "Southie" had been developed for Middle-Class WASPs. When the WASPs moved to Back Bay, Irish Catholics moved in. Nowadays, the parish congregation was English-and Spanish-speaking.

The cathedral was in the Gothic Revival style, built from Roxbury puddingstone with gray limestone trim. It was 364 feet long, 90 feet wide, and 120 feet tall. It held about 2,000 worshipers at any one time. It was most famous for Cardinal Cushing's requiem mass for President Kennedy, broadcast to the nation, and using Mozart's *Requiem*, played by the Boston Symphony Orchestra.

Less well-known is its insane, stupid, maddening bureaucracy.

While on the phone, Pearson had been shuttled around from the receptionist to secretary to church secretary, to priest, to yet another priest, back to another secretary.

Then we actually arrived at the diocesan office.

And the dance began anew.

After the first twenty minutes in the waiting room, I sat down, pulled out my rosary, and started praying. I intended to ask that I could fulfill whatever purpose God wanted me to serve. I asked that I have the energy and strength to see through the end of God's mission that day. Every mission I had been on with Pearson had been a mess. First London had been threatened with destruction. Then all of Europe had been threatened with an army of demons. And now America would be threatened with ... what?

On the law of averages, I didn't think the threat level would be *down*graded. We had already realized that we had at least a squad of the possessed kicking around the area. Where they were or who they were wasn't even the problem. The true problem was the question none of us could answer: what could anyone need nearly a dozen possessed for? One possessed psycho had been enough to start a prison riot in Rikers that threatened to overwhelm the city and over ten thousand prisoners in the jail itself. What would ten do? And was ten the upper limit that had been unleashed?

I sat while Father Pearson bargained for our entry. At the side table next to me were rainbow-colored pamphlets. The initials on the front were L.G.B.T.T.Q.Q.I.A.A.P. I knew from time spent in New York's Greenwich Village that it stood for "lesbian, gay, bisexual, transgender, transsexual, queer, questioning, intersex, asexual, ally, pansexual."

I was taken aback by the presence of any material in a Bishop's office with the word "sexual" on the front cover, to heck with this.

I picked it up and opened it...

I stopped paying attention after the term "pedophobia" was used. And no, it wasn't being used to mean "fear of children." (Though I knew more people who were scared of children then they were by pedophiles—most of the people I knew were more likely to break the legs of a pedophile than be scared of them).

I palmed all of the pamphlets and stuck them in my pocket. I'd be sure to recycle them into something more interesting later on.

I went back to my rosary.

After the first six decades (which is sixty Hail Marys, and a dozen Our Fathers), I paused and switched to Psalm 17. It felt right for dealing with a bureaucracy.

Hear, LORD, my plea for justice; pay heed to my cry; Listen to my prayer from lips without guile. From you let my vindication come; your eyes see what is right. You have tested my heart, searched it in the night. You have tried me by fire, but find no malice in me. My mouth has not transgressed as others often do. As your lips have instructed me, I have kept from the way of the lawless. My steps have kept to your paths; my feet have not faltered.

I call upon you; answer me, O God. Turn your ear to me; hear my speech. Show your wonderful mercy, you who deliver with your right arm those who seek refuge from their foes. Keep me as the apple of your eye; hide me in the shadow of your wings from the wicked who despoil me. My ravenous enemies press upon me; they close their hearts, they fill their mouths with proud roaring.

My thoughts were interrupted by Father Pearson demanding, "Would you like the Pope to visit your cathedral?"

My eyes opened at that. Even the priest, who had arrived while I was lost in prayer, blanched. When Pope Pius XIII was first inaugurated, he went on a world tour. During every press conference, he would greet everyone similarly... until the Pope personally knocked the teeth out of a priest's mouth. The cops were usually waiting in the wings to take the victim of the assault away on charges ranging from sexual abuse to embezzling, and any other crime he could find. No one was safe, from lay secretaries to Cardinals. Pius XIII had elevated street-level priests to high office and sent those in high office to jail. Some people wanted him to clean up the red tape. Instead, he cleaned house.

It was half-past four when the priest emerged from the Bishop's rooms and said that we could enter.

Bishop Robert Ashley had been installed by Pius XIII's predecessor. He had not endeared himself to anyone. During the press conference where the Pope shook his hand, the grip looked particularly tight, and so did Ashley's smile. But Ashley had held onto his purple robes and the ring. He hadn't been fired, but he hadn't been quite the media darling he had been before the latest Pope had been elected.

Ashley looked like a less photogenic Benedict Cumberbatch. He had a broad forehead perfect for head-butting, and a weak, narrow chin I could have used for a blunt object. His eyes were a pale blue, with the black of the pupil leaking into the iris. He wore his Bishopric robes indoors, even though it wasn't a public event.

Ashley tried to sound welcoming as he greeted us. "Hello. How can we help you folks?"

Pearson stepped forward, looking angrier than I had ever seen him. "We aren't *folks*. I have been sent by Auxiliary Bishop Xavier O'Brien in Rome to investigate the slaughter of an entire monastery, and you have us cooling our heels outside while you're in here playing silly buggers. And these two fine gentlemen are from the police, here to help me. We need to know every referral you've made in reference to exorcism in the past month or three. For starters. Especially every last person you have ever referred to the monastery out in Marblehead."

Ashley looked at us a moment, then laughed in our faces. "Oh, we don't believe in demons *here*. We are a *modern* church, without any of that silly superstitious nonsense."

I kept praying the rosary to keep my cool and not do something I might regret.

Alex, however, did not take it as placidly as I did. He leaned forward, slammed his hands on the table in a deliberate attempt to make enough noise to rattle the Bishop's marbles lose. "Are you kidding me? You're turning wine into blood on behalf of God, who became a person, died and came back from the dead, and you're going to tell me that *demons* are the part you can't wrap your tiny little brain around?"

Ashley waved his hands in dismissal. "Oh, we're not changing anything from wine. That's just in memoriam."

At that, my eyes opened in surprise. Pearson audibly gasped. And while we were shocked to heck and back, Alex reached over the desk, grabbed Bishop Ashley by the collar, and pulled him upright, then proceeded to shake him like a rag doll. *"That's Protestant dogma, you schmuck! I'm not religious, and even I know the difference!"*

Bishop Ashley flailed at Alex's hands, and Alex upgraded his aggression from the Bishop's collar to his hands on his throat. The grip was firm but not enough to kill the Bishop outright—not yet, anyway.

"Stop him!" Ashley begged.

Alex kept shaking the Bishop and snapped, "Tell us who you sent to the monastery, you idiot."

"Minniva! Minniva Atwood!"

Alex stopped choking him and threw the Bishop back into his chair. Alex pointed at him like a gun. "You are going to get your secretary's ass in here, and you are going to get us her address, or by all that's holy, I am going to beat you black and blue."

Ashley opened his mouth to say something to Alex but stopped and looked at us. "Are you going to let him bully me around like that?"

Pearson shrugged. "I'm sorry, was I supposed to stop him? I'm just a priest. Though I will be *happy* to report *all* of this to the Pope. He will be thrilled to *death* with the news of how helpful you've been."

Alex snapped, "Address! Now!"

Pearson hovered over Bishop Ashley while Alex loomed at the back of the room. I calmly and casually strolled over to his side and whispered, "Really? Little much, wasn't it?"

Alex looked from the Bishop to me and back again. "It wasn't an act. I can't believe this dickless wonder can't believe in the supernatural when that's literally *his job.* I've seen too much of this crap to listen to his BS. My God, man, you have some stupid people in your hierarchy."

I shrugged. I knew the history of our hierarchy. There were moments where God needed to give a stern talking to Saint Peter, Pope number one. I didn't hold out much hope that the rest of the hierarchy would do a lot better. "No argument."

I wandered the back of the office as we waited for the secretary to give us the address for Minniva Atwood. There were pamphlets on one of the side tables. It was for the "Women's Health Corps, Boston."

My blood went cold at the name of the death cult that had tried to slaughter my entire family twice. I was about to throw the pamphlets at the Bishop and follow through on every threat Alex had in mind – then I saw the date. The most recent pamphlet was two years old. It predated the arrest and prosecution of the entire WHC.

But on the back of the pamphlet, in small print, read the copyright on the pamphlet itself. It was the logo of the company than printed the PR materials. It was a giant "M" with the last leg of the letter turning into an "I."

I swept up all of the WHC pamphlets and put them on the table in a stack. Then I pulled out all of the L.G.B.T.Q.M.O.U.S.E. pamphlets from outside in the hallway.

They had also been printed by Matchett Industrial.

"Father Pearson," I called back, "I think we have a problem."

Pearson and Alex swapped places. Bishop Ashley whimpered. I pointed out the content of the pamphlets, then the logo.

Pearson glanced at me and turned back to the Bishop. "What is your relationship with Matchett Industrial?"

Ashley whimpered a little when Alex raised the back of his hand as if to strike him. "He donates to the church! Lots of money!"

I arched a brow and spared Pearson a glance. I said, "That's funny, coming from a big Boston company, isn't it?"

Ashley held up his hands. "He earmarks it for the causes he cares about. Needle exchange! Housing for the undocumented. He asks that we put out pamphlets."

I didn't even ask which pamphlets. But something felt off about Matchett's donations. "Needle exchange, but not your drug support groups?"

Ashley nodded eagerly, happy to answer my question – it meant that Alex took a step back. "Right."

He wants to continue the problem, not fix it, I thought. "Any *particular* undocumented?"

Ashley floundered for a moment and reached for a drawer. Alex leaned forward over him, in case there was a weapon. Ashley grabbed a folder and tossed it on the desk. "Photos. From our support group."

I grabbed it and opened it.

The first picture – the *very* first picture – was a group shot. The timestamp put it as three years ago.

Three things struck me immediately.

One. They were all Hispanic. All of them. This may not surprise you, but not all "undocumented" were Hispanic. In Boston, many were Irish. The odds of them being only Hispanic were stacked against it.

Two. Everyone in the photograph was heavily tattooed. Everyone had at least one tattoo with a giant "13" on it. Meaning they were all MS-13, a street gang that had expanded so that they were one part cartel and one part terrorist group.

Three. Right in the middle of it, the man in the exact center, was a man I knew. He had been a shot caller for MS-13 until he went into Rikers, and then a padded cell, before finally being ripped apart by shadows. His name had been Rene Ormeno, and he and his men had tried to murder me repeatedly.

"Sumbitch," I whispered.

At that moment, the secretary came back with an addressed for Minniva Atwood. But just as importantly, he had her job details. She was chief of sales for Matchett Industrial.

WE PULLED UP TO THE HOUSE AT THE EDGE OF BOSTON AND found three black vans parked in front. One of them had cut off the driveway, and another was parked on the lawn, back facing us. It had no license plates. At the end of the driveway, two large hulking men in Secret Service chic were carrying a slender brunette. It was Minniva Atwood. We knew thanks to the description a suddenly-helpful secretary had provided us at the diocesan office. Slender, broad-shouldered, and physically active, she put up a good fight. Her shoulder-length dark brown hair and smart business attire were in disarray, giving witness to her efforts. She kicked and struggled against them, screaming her head off. Without hesitation, I gunned the engine and turned the wheel.

My wheels went up the next driveway over. We cut across the lawn next door and shot into Minniva's driveway. The two men holding her didn't have time to react. One held Minniva with one arm and reached inside his jacket with the other for his gun. The other one looked too confused to react.

I twisted the wheel just enough to shoot past Minniva and slammed into the man in black. I slammed on the brakes as the car passed behind Minniva. The gunman was knocked away from Minniva and went flying into the closed door of her garage. I spun the wheel as we slowed, bringing the passenger side around to face Minniva and her other kidnapper. Alex jammed his gun out the window, into the kidnapper's face, and fired four rounds. Minniva screamed and ducked her head away from the noise and spatter erupting from the ruined face.

Pearson got out of the back seat and grabbed Minniva by the arms. "Come with us if you want to live!" he called to her as he hustled her into the back of the car.

The men from the cars threw the doors open and stormed out. They weren't armed with anything visible, which made me wonder how much they had up their sleeves. The driveway was still blocked.

Not wanting to get into a game of chicken with the gunmen, I spun the wheel and threw the car into reverse, backing down the driveway and dashing into the backyard.

I slid out of the car and shouted at them, "Get into the house. I'll hold them off."

"With what?" Alex screamed, incredulous. "You have body armor we don't know about?"

I smiled at him and let it happen.

Under my shirt, the clay armor around my chest sprang to life. Sheets of clay armor telescoped out over my body. Interlocking plates slid down my arms and legs while the helmet slid up over my head, then the face mask locked into position.

Alex blinked. Then shrugged. "Yeah. Sure. Of course. Clay powered armor. Because I'm in a comic book now." He threw open his door and held his gun up as Pearson and Minniva ran behind him.

The garage door exploded open. The kidnapper I struck with the car stepped out and turned to me. His black sunglasses were broken, one lens entirely ripped off. It revealed one solid glowing red eye.

I leaped forward in my golem armor and crashed into the man in black. While the power suit made me look light and nimble, I easily weighed four hundred pounds.

The kidnapper only staggered back a few steps. He reared back and swung for me. I deflected the blow with my left hand and shot in with my right. My fist came in low, diving into his stomach. It slid him back along the concrete without doing anything else to him.

The entire time, his face was impassive, as though he were bored.

Okay. Not human. Check. Not even a little. Good.

He darted in again. I sidestepped the charge, then grabbed his right wrist with both hands. I pulled back as he kept running. His entire body weight went one way while his arm went another. It was enough to break bone in a normal person. As I drove his arm to the ground, his feet went out from under him. I clomped down on his chest, held my grip on his arm, and *pulled*. It was a move meant to dislocate the shoulder of a human. I gave it everything the armor had.

His arm came right out of its socket with a sound like breaking stone.

Instead of blood and bone, the open wound poured forth a green gelatinous substance. I dropped the arm and backed away from it, not wanting to get too close.

I looked up. The other kidnappers filled the driveway. There were fourteen of them to block my path. The augmented reality of the armor's vision scanned over them once, then again. The last time penetrated the glamour they hid behind.

They were less human and more ... scaley. Some sort of serpent men.

Snakes. Why did it have to be snakes?

Their steps even now encircle me; they watch closely, keeping low to the ground, like lions eager for prey, like a young lion lurking in ambush.

I reached down for the driveway and grabbed either side of the slab of concrete in front of me. With the powered grip of the armor, I ripped the concrete from the ground, hefted it, and hurled it at the line of attack like a death Frisbee. Some ducked, some dove out of the way. Five of them weren't fast enough and were cut in half.

Rise, O LORD, confront and cast them down;

They were so busy with the incoming slab that they didn't see that I leaped right behind it.

I landed on the head of one of those that dove, pulping his skull. I spun, delivering a right stone hammer fist to the nearest temple. The head caved in, and the neck snapped to one side.

At the same time, I jabbed a left knife-hand into a serpent man's throat. I punctured the skin and came out the other side, then chopped away. I ripped out the side of his neck, casting away green goo from within.

The remaining serpents jumped me, piling onto me like I was in a football game.

Rescue my soul from the wicked.

I found purchase on the ground and pushed up with all my strength. I pushed up, to my feet, throwing off all of the serpents.

Slay them with your sword; with your hand, LORD, slay them;

One serpent landed in front of me, bouncing back to his scaley feet. He threw his head back, and I instinctively ducked. He spat for me, where my head was. His spit landed in the face of the serpent behind me. On contact, there was the spit-sizzle of acid melting away flesh. The serpent man screamed and grabbed his face as it melted off.

Snatch them from the world in their prime. Their bellies are being filled with your friends; their children are satisfied too, for they share what is left with their young.

The serpent before me opened his mouth again, but before he could rear back for another load, I sprang up and forward, fist cocked back.

I am just.

I punched right down his throat and out the back of his head. I swung back, ripping the serpent's head off, hurling it at another creature.

Let me see your face.

I whirled on the remaining five creatures. A window opened

from the house behind them, and Alex casually threw a package of thermite onto one of them. The package broke open against its head, opening it up to the air. The oxygen ignited a chemical inside, which set off the thermite. He burst into flame, and the others fled from the fire.

I grabbed the one straggler who darted down the driveway. Alex fired into the other three. I took the straggler by the neck, lifted him over my head, then threw him into the concrete, head first. The head exploded like a balloon filled with green Jello. There didn't even seem to be a brain inside the skull, just animating fluids.

When I awake, let me be filled with your presence.

The final three tried to flee. Alex gunned down one of them in the back, felling him.

I leapt onto their backs, driving them to the concrete. With balled fists, I pounded down on their skulls like I hammered a nail. After half a dozen strikes, the heads were pulped and gushing ooze.

I pushed off of the bodies, to my feet. With a flick of my wrists, I rid myself of the spatter. I thought at the golem armor for more data. The display flicked to a green tint, giving me the all-clear.

I looked down at the serpent men. The display on the helmet highlighted the green slime and blinked for a moment. The data filed down the right side of my helmet's vision, studying the goo. "The suit says that they were animated by ectoplasm. Apparently, that's what happens with a ... summoned construct. I guess that means they were demonic flesh robots."

Alex leaned out the window and looked at me like this was boring. "Yay. Can we leave now?"

"Excuse me, we have a problem!" Father Pearson called out from the back.

Alex rolled his eyes. "Of course, we do."

I powered down the armor and slid it away so it folded back under my clothing. Alex pulled himself back inside. I took the short route, grabbed the window sill and pulled myself inside the house.

Minniva Atwood, lay boneless in Pearson's arms. Her eyes were wide awake and staring, almost like she was catatonic. But her hand reached out to me, and her mouth moved, wordlessly asking for help.

"What's wrong with her?" I asked.

Pearson glanced my way. "The demon has rendered her mute."

Normal operating procedure would have been to spend *hours* talking with the police about everything we had done at the house and everything that had led us up to that point. We would be grilled by a rotating set of police officers for hours on end to make certain the stories we told were all in sync. Minniva Atwood would be dragged off to a hospital and probably a psych ward. Alex's gun would be disappeared into a box, then a lab, then a report would be filed with the NYPD, and he would spend the better part of the next week without a gun, and being questions by Internal Affairs of New York, as well as the investigators from Boston.

If we were lucky, standard operating procedure would keep us penned up tight, and out of circulation for the better part of two weeks. Perhaps more.

With that in mind, I looked at Alex and Pearson. "We're getting out of here immediately. Throw her in the back of the car. Want me to carry?"

Pearson rose with her in his arms. She was long, but slender. And he had been a spy and who knew what else. She wasn't a problem for him. And the demon wasn't fighting. Then again, given what Pearson said earlier about demons not wanting to tip their hand by revealing themselves, that could be the demon playing it safe. The longer it could drag this out and prevent us from talking to Minniva, the less time we would have.

I armored up and led the way outside in case something closed in on us between the time we left the house and the time we pulled out. I didn't know the range on the armor, and I wasn't going to spend time asking.

I got out of the house and circled in front of the car. No one was there. As Alex and Pearson loaded Minniva in the car, I peeked around the corner of the house, down the driveway.

There were no intruders around. But even stranger, there weren't any of the serpent men either. Both the bodies and the clothes on them had melted away, leaving a little bit of a wet stain where the attackers had been. At least they were self-cleaning.

If we allowed ourselves to be detained by the cops, that would make things even *more* complicated. Questions like "Why did you fire your gun?" or "Why is there a slab of concrete ripped out of the driveway?" would be inconvenient.

It took me a moment to piece together why the serpent men had melted. The golem armor had told me that they were summoned constructs and animated by ectoplasm. Apparently, when they were defeated, the summoned were cast back into the pit from which they came.

I armored down, got behind the wheel, and made our way out of the driveway. I casually drove away, under the speed limit, drawing no attention to us.

Alex kept his gun in his lap the entire time, his head on a swivel. I had to admit that my eyes were on a fast rotating schedule, from my mirrors to the windshield and back again. Pearson sat in the back, and he held Minniva, keeping her calm, peacefully reciting the Rite of exorcism.

"Don't you have an app for that sort of thing?" Alex asked.

I spared him a glance. "What sort of thing?"

"Demonic whatever the Hell they were. It was disorienting when you squashed their heads and they're empty except for Jello. But you have a magic ring for that, don't you?"

I took a deep breath and calmed myself. "One, it's not magic. Any more than the Ark of the Covenant or the Holy Grail would be magic. Second, do you know why I don't use bilocation to stay home while I'm off getting shot at?"

Alex shrugged. "I have no idea. I always wondered."

I took a deep, calming breath. After all, it wasn't self-evident to everyone. "We're a few steps beyond 'With Great power comes Great Responsibility.' These are gifts from God. I ask for what I need. I don't say 'I'm going to do this because I want to.' I use what I need and no more than what I need. If God were going to do every last little thing, then I don't need free will, He could just pull the strings. Heck, He wouldn't even need me. God may have whispered in the ear of King David to take down Goliath with a slingshot, but David still needed years in the fields practicing and taking out wolves. I have powered armor, and I have charisms out my ears. I want to save the ring for when I need it."

Alex said nothing for a long stretch as he thought it over. "You could have just said you were saving your ammo."

I scoffed. "That would be too certain an answer. I don't know how this works. I don't know if there is a charge for it. It may be that it can never run out of charge. The Jihadi thugs who shot at me had bits of the Soul Stone embedded in them and ran on hate. I never got to see them with constant, prolonged use of their powers. They also had the main stone within proximity. So there are more variables than I feel comfortable experimenting with, especially during a firefight."

Alex sighed and leaned back in his chair. "You manage to make everything so over-complicated."

I laughed. "If my life were simple, we wouldn't be in this mess."

Alex shrugged. "So, where are we going? We need to get the demon out of her, right?"

"We at least need to suppress it," Pearson told us.

I nodded. "That's why I'm going back to the summer house. Sinead has a basement and a guest bed. We can tie her down in case things go bad. And they'll ask a lot fewer questions than a hotel would when the screaming starts."

Alex rolled his eyes. "And you don't think this is a case for using the ring because?"

"You heard Pearson. Combat exorcism leaves the possessed worn out and exhausted, and risks even more spiritual and psychological damage. Miss Atwood there is probably on our side. Let's not torture our friends any more than we have to, okay?"

"Hey, if I weren't a masochist, would I still be your partner?" Alex looked back at Pearson. "Now, let me get this straight, she's not saying anything, and that's the demon's fault."

Pearson nodded at Alex. He waited to say "Amen" before adding, "Many demons are mute."

Alex arched a brow. "Really? That's the biggest party trick it has?"

"It doesn't need much more than that to thwart us, does it?"

Pearson sighed. "Like I said before, usually, demons try *not* to manifest. It's considered a failure if a priest draws it out and gets a reaction. When there are several demons in a body, the weak one comes out first."

I nearly hit the breaks and pulled over. I kept my calm and continued driving evenly. I felt Alex tense up next to me. We had fought Christopher Curran and the legion of demons inside of him.

But if Pearson was accurate, then we only interacted with the *weakest* of the demons. And that one had nearly killed us both. *I may be getting to work out the ring like Alex wants. Though I don't think it's going to make things that much easier.*

Pearson continued: "But right now, the demon is doing the minimum to keep us from talking with Minniva. Which means that whatever is happening is so important that a demon is violating normal behavior to keep this a secret. Every minute that we're delayed is a minute we're kept from finding out whatever is happening."

I drove faster. "Alex, text Mariel. Tell her we've got incoming."

Alex gave me a look. "You're kidding me. We are not taking six levels of possessed to the same place where your *kids and wife* live, right?"

I glanced at Alex. "Maybe you'd like to bring her to Bishop Ashley's church? Maybe he'll change his tune if we bring the woman we saved from the demonic gunman into his church. And then he *won't* call the police. I'm sure we can roll the dice, and at least one of the priests *under* Bishop Ashley would believe what we're doing."

Alex frowned. "Okay. Maybe you have a point."

When we got to the house, I pulled up almost to the door, on the walkway. Mariel and Sinead came out of the house and opened the back car door. They helped Pearson carry Minniva into the house. Alex and I were hot on their heels and got her down into the basement. We placed her on the bed in the basement. Pearson went to work praying over Minniva, with Alex behind him, hand on his gun.

Mariel, however, waved me out of the room.

"Hey, hon," she started sweetly. "What's with the girl?"

I shrugged. "She's possessed. At least *she* wants the demon out."

Mariel paused, blinked, then held up a hand. "Wait. Hold up. Go back. She's possessed?"

I nodded. "Not sure how. But she went to the monastery to get an exorcism. Then the monastery got slaughtered, and some heavies tried to kidnap her from her home."

Mariel frowned. "This isn't another cult, is it?"

I shrugged. "I honestly don't know. It almost sounds like it has to be. This many demons? It has to be deliberate."

"*I SAID SPEAK*," Pearson roared behind us in the next room over. There was a hissing sound. Alex cocked his gun.

I sighed and kissed Mariel on the forehead. "I'm sorry, honey. I think I have to go suppress a demon."

Mariel sighed. "At least come up for dinner. Secure her, come up in thirty minutes, eat, come back?"

I smiled at her. "That's a deal. See you in thirty."

I walked back into the basement bedroom as Minniva Atwood lunged for Pearson's throat. I darted in and caught her around the waist when she was in midair. I thought at the armor around my chest and summoned up a helmet. I was just in time as Minniva elbowed me in the back of the head. I tossed her back on the bed and armored up the rest of the way, just in case she wanted to start something.

Pearson kept praying. "Most glorious Prince of the Heavenly Armies, Saint Michael the Archangel, defend us in our battle against principalities and powers, against the rulers of this world of darkness, against the spirits of wickedness in the high places."

Minniva suddenly started coughing. It was a light cough at first, just trying to clear her throat.

"Come to the assistance of men whom God has created to His likeness and whom He has redeemed at a great price from the tyranny of the devil."

Minniva's cough became heavier. Maybe she needed a glass of water.

"The Holy Church venerates you as her guardian and protector; to you, the Lord has entrusted the souls of the redeemed to be led into heaven. Pray therefore the God of Peace to crush Satan beneath our feet, that he may no longer retain men captive and do injury to the Church."

The coughs increased so much I thought it sounded like some food went down the wrong way. The coughing paused so she could yawn. The first yawn was like a need for a little extra oxygen.

"Offer our prayers to the Most High! That without delay they may draw His mercy down upon us; take hold of the dragon, the old serpent, which is the Devil and Satan. Bind him and cast him into the bottomless pit that he may no longer seduce the nations!"

Minniva's next yawn was longer and deeper, like she couldn't breathe enough.

Pearson continued. "In the Name of Jesus Christ, our God and Lord, strengthened by the intercession of the Immaculate Virgin Mary, Mother of God, of Blessed Michael the Archangel, of the Blessed Apostles Peter and Paul and all the Saints. and powerful in the holy authority of our ministry, we confidently undertake to repulse the attacks and deceits of the devil."

Minniva bent over and hacked and coughed like she was trying to dislodge a bone in her throat. She doubled over.

"God arises; His enemies are scattered, and those who hate Him flee before Him. As smoke is driven away, so are they driven; as wax melts before the fire, so the wicked perish at the presence of God. Behold the Cross of the Lord, flee bands of enemies. The Lion of the tribe of Judah, the offspring of David, hath conquered. May Thy mercy, Lord, descend upon us. As great as our hope in Thee."

Minniva vomited on the floor. I reflexively backed up and away, so I wouldn't get it on my shoes, despite my new armor.

"We drive you from us, whoever you may be, unclean spirits, all satanic powers, all—

Minniva growled and hurled herself at me, slamming me aside like she was the rugby fullback, and I was a twig. She whirled on Father Pearson and threw herself at him in full rage.

In mid-air, Minniva slammed up against the wall. She was horizontal to the floor. She thrashed against restraints that I couldn't see. The display on the golem helmet highlighted a string in the air holding her to the wall.

I followed the threads back ... to Lena.

Lena stood there in her pink dress. Her mouth was in a straight line, her brows furrowed.

"—infernal invaders, all wicked legions, assemblies and sects," Pearson continued without missing a beat.

"Hussar," Lena said casually. "Will you come and play with me and Jeremy? We're playing Legos."

I smiled. Jeremy had single-handedly built up his own Death Star without a kit. He had shared the joy of interlocking plastic blocks with his new sister.

"Maybe later, if you don't mind. We have to kick the Hell out of a demon."

Lena smiled. She flung Minniva Atwood back to the bed. "Can I watch?"

I turned to Minniva to make sure she wasn't going anywhere. She twisted to the floor and vomited up ... sea foam, apparently. "You have to promise to leave if it gets too scary."

Alex scoffed. "Does that mean I can be excused now?"

I rolled my eyes. I was about to answer Alex when I noted that everything she vomited up melted away, as if into nothing.

"In the Name and by the power of Our Lord Jesus Christ," Pearson continued. "May you be snatched away and driven from the Church of God and from the souls made to the image and likeness of God and redeemed by the Precious Blood of the Divine Lamb. Most cunning serpent, you shall no more dare to deceive the human race, persecute the Church, torment God's elect and sift them as wheat."

Minniva pushed up and tried to launch herself again. She faltered and fell over, vomiting up nails.

Then in clicked. In Germany, I had been cursed by some neon anti-Pope satanist band leader. I had coughed up nails. It was a way to show that the curse was being expelled.

As Minniva continued with coughing up bowed ribbons, I thought, *This girl is cursed six ways to Sunday.*

I tuned out some of Pearson's ritual, and came back in time to hear: "Thus, cursed dragon, and you, diabolical legions, we adjure you by the living God, by the true God, by the holy God, by the God who so loved the world that He gave up His only Son, that every soul believing in Him might not perish but have life everlasting, stop deceiving human creatures and pouring out to them the poison of eternal damnation; stop harming the Church and hindering her liberty. Begone, Satan, inventor and master of all deceit, enemy of man's salvation."

Minniva was sweating now.

I glanced at my watch and winced. I had promised Mariel that I would be up and ready for dinner.

"Lena, let me know when you get bored or scared. I'll come down and swap with you. I need to head up. Are you going to be okay?"

Lena gave me a beatific little smile. "Of course, Hussar."

I armored down. I didn't want to surprise Mariel. I had shown her the new party trick only once to explain what the golem armor did. Wearing it to the dining room table just seemed rude.

The table was fully loaded when I got there. Sinead, Mariel, and Jeremy waited.

"Family meeting?" I asked. "I missed the memo."

"We should all be on the same page," Mariel said from the counter. "So sit and start talking."

I WALKED THE THREE OF THEM THROUGH THE DAY THUS FAR.
The monastery led to Downey. Downey led to the Bishop's office.
The Bishop led to Minniva.

Is that all I did today? I thought. *I feel like I got more done when I
was shoveling through paperwork.*

There was a loud clomping sound coming up the basement stairs
that I easily recognized as "petulant child." Lena stepped into the
dining doom and said, "They're done. It ended kinda boring."

"Do they need me down there?" I asked.

Lena shrugged. "I don't know." She walked over next to Jeremy
and was about to speak when something caught her eyes. She stabbed
the table with her finger, pointing at the business card of Gerald
Downey. Her fingernail jabbed into the M with the I at the end of it.

"I know them!" Lena declared. "That was in the truck." She
looked at me, excited. "Remember when you found me? That truck!"

My stomach sank. The truck she referred to had been filled with
men women and children designated to be sex slaves, trafficked by a
succubus and a small army of Jihadis.

"I don't remember seeing it," I told her.

She frowned, then looked embarrassed. "I made a mess over it."

I said nothing. The mess she had made in the truck wasn't an accident of excrement, but a mess that literally caused heads to explode. She probably meant that the Matchett Industries logo had been covered by brain matter.

Jeremy reached over and slid the card so he could read it. He looked at it and frowned. "I think I know this one too." He looked to Mariel. "Mom. Remember that stupid course about sex?"

Mariel's face hardened. "The one with the pictures? Several years ago?"

Jeremy nodded. "These were on the textbooks."

I raised a brow, looking back and forth. "Someone want to tell me?"

Mariel sighed. "Someone tried to sell Jerry's school a collection of sex ed books. They were ... graphic. Very graphic. And they went beyond sex."

I arched a brow. "Should I ask."

Jeremy shrugged. "Men making out. Blech."

I took a slow breath. Five seconds to breathe in. Three seconds to breathe out. I did it again. And again. "And no one told me this ... why?"

"I got them arrested for showing porn to minors," Mariel answered. "It was during the Curran thing. You were busy. And you were beaten up a lot. I handled it. It was a program under Mayor Hoynes. You got rid of him. I figured the problem was solved. I didn't think it was a bigger problem than that."

I nodded slowly, still annoyed. I would have cursed myself for having been out of the loop. But I had spent a lot of time laid up after I arrested Curran. She had good reason for keeping me out of it.

Lena, however, seemed bored by the discussion. She looked at Jeremy. "Legos?"

Jeremy's eyes lit up. "Legos!"

Lena and Jeremy darted out of the dining room and upstairs.

Once their elephantine clomping faded away, I heard the slow, patient footsteps from the basement stairs.

Mariel, Sinead, and I rose from the table.

We all converged on the basement door. Pearson held Minniva's hand as he helped her up the stairs. Alex came up close behind them, afraid that Minniva would fall back.

It was an easy mistake to make. She looked like she had been through the ringer.

"Is she safe?" Sinead asked. She and Mariel were on either side of the door, and ready to reach down and help them up.

Pearson smiled at them faintly. He didn't look too hot, either. He was still worn out after the first Exorcism. He didn't look that good after his second one of the day, either. "It's all right. She accepted a host. Soul food, if you will."

I swear I did not hit him for that pun. But I didn't scold Alex for smacking him upside the head for it, either.

I reached down and for Minniva's free hand. "Miss Atwood?"

She absently took it, then looked up at my hand, and then at my face, like I had mysteriously appeared from the mists. "Hello?"

I held my sigh. *She's gonna be out of it for a while.*

She took my hand and grasped at the rough sensation of the scar in my palm.

I helped pull her up the stairs. "Miss Atwood, my name is Detective Thomas Nolan. I understand that you were trying to reach a Passionist monastery in regards to demonic possession?"

Minniva's eyes focused on me. Her gaze narrowed. She was pissed. Thankfully, not at me. "Yes. Yes, I did. But I don't know who I could..."

She drifted off as she stepped into the light of the kitchen. She looked around at all of us and saw our faces—in particular, our lack of surprise. She looked to the priest and focused.

"You know, don't you? You know that there's something out there."

Alex scoffed as he came up. "Lady, you don't know the half of what we've seen."

Still gently holding one hand, I led her to the dining room. I met Mariel's eye, then casually jerked my head over to the platter of food on the counter. Minniva Atwood may have been a natural twig with the bone structure of a bird, but she'd had a hard day. She needed to eat. "Now, please, let's get you fed, and then you can tell us what happened?"

It took a few minutes, but once Minniva had a bit of food in her, she was more than happy to talk.

"It may have been four or five months ago," she began, "but the Vice President of Human Resources, Herbert West, wanted to have a team-building exercise at Matchett Industrial—you know I work there, right?"

I nodded. "We know."

Minniva frowned. "Okay. Well, he wanted a team-building exercise during the state of the company meeting."

Alex raised his hand to interrupt. "A state of the what-now? Sorry, I've never had a real job. I'm just a cop."

Minniva smiled a little. "It's *supposed* to be..." She sighed and shook her head. "It's a Dilbert comedy routine as a documentary. In company speak, the meeting is ..." She paused, translating from normal into bureaucrat in her head. "An opportunity for leadership to share the vision of the company, so they can move the organization forward and hit desired growth goals. The leaders talk about where the company has been, where it is, successes won, challenges overcome, mistakes made or path corrections, and where the company is going. So that everyone is on the same page, marching towards the same goals, and they know their role in making that vision a reality. It's motivating to know how your work plays into the big picture. The fastest way to get from Point A to Point B is if everyone is rowing in the same direction. But your people need to know where to row to if they are going to contribute."

When she finished, she broke up laughing. She laughed a little too hard and a little too long. *I hope it's just stress.*

When she settled down, she waved it away. "It's a pep talk everyone is required to go to. Long boring speeches broken up by entertainment and food."

I looked around at everyone else, who seemed as confused as I felt. I shrugged. "Okay. What about it?"

"VP West talked everyone into a 'mass' as a 'team-building' exercise for the state of the company meeting this year."

I braced myself for the worst. Sinead, however, shrugged, and said, "That doesn't seem bad. A mass? Sounds like the sort of thing Hobby Lobby should do. They're Christian."

Minniva stared at Sinead for a moment before realizing she needed to clarify. "A black mass."

Alex slapped the table as he leaned forward and spat out, "A *what?*"

"Satanic ritual," Pearson stated flatly. "It's an inversion of the actual mass. Unsurprisingly, popularized by the French. It's the sort of thing you get in early and high-level Freemasonry. Satan as the god of reason and the opponent of Christianity. Or just straight-up witch-craft. It really depends on the location and the purpose of the one holding the ritual."

It didn't take much for me to put two and two together. "That's how you were possessed."

Minniva nodded. "Yes. None of us were allowed to leave. It was mandatory. And I didn't think it could do that much harm if I slept through it."

Sinead asked, "What changed?"

"After a few days, I couldn't eat. I couldn't sleep. I had mood swings. I had memory problems. I thought it was stress and depression."

Pearson's eyes narrowed. "Then it got worse."

Minniva nodded. "Yes. It was almost like my house was haunted.

Footsteps in the empty house. Screams in the night like they were next to my ears. My cell phone became useless. Then ..." She drifted off, then reached down to her sleeve cuff and rolled it back. While her skin was pale white, her forearms were solid bruises.

Alex frowned. "We didn't do that. Right?"

Minniva shook her head. "This was a week ago."

Sinead leaned forward to get a better look. "Looks fresh to me."

Minniva rolled the sleeve back down, gingerly. "I know. It never healed. And I started thinking ... things."

We waited for a long moment, hoping that Minniva would fill in the silence of her own accord. But she bowed her head, and harshly whispered, "Please don't make me tell you."

Pearson answered. "You thought about hurting people. Killing people. Maybe even yourself. Unnatural thoughts about children, or other women. When you were allowed to sleep, you had nightmares about any or all of the above."

Minniva looked up at him like he was the magician. "How did you know?"

Pearson shrugged. "This is my day job. Symptoms of possession are like a disease."

Minniva took a deep, shuddering breath and let it out slowly. "I went to doctors. I went to shrinks. Everyone was ready to put me on pills. But I can't do my job when I'm drugged up to my eyeballs. But then, I found I couldn't pray. That's when I knew I needed to talk to someone. I eventually ended up at the monastery. I told them everything I knew. I even gave them names of people at the state of the company meeting."

Alex held up his hand. "Excuse me. One second. Hold on." He pointed at Minniva. "A state of the company meeting?" He looked around at Sinead, Pearson, and me. "We pieced together maybe, what? Ten people at the crime scene?" He looked back to Minniva. "A state of the company meeting with only ten people?"

Minniva blinked and shook her head. "No, you don't understand.

Those are just the names from the meeting I *remember*. It may have been the entire company."

The entire table went silent. If the entire company had gone bad —dragged into a black mass—that was hundreds if not thousands of people. Each and every one of them could have had the power of Gerald Downey—assuming that Downey wasn't the *weakest* among them.

After the long, long pause, Alex said, "I'm going back to New York now."

I didn't contradict him. I looked at Pearson and said, "May we chat in the other room a moment?"

We walked into the kitchen. I raised a hand. "Item one, I think we're going to need an overnight delivery."

Pearson arched a brow. He paused for a long moment, pondering what I could need to send away for. "What did you have in mind?"

I told him. He thought it over a minute, then nodded. He pulled out his phone and sent a text message. "It's done. What next?"

"Start with VP HR Herbert West. That name sounds familiar."

Pearson nodded. "Lovecraft character. Created his own science-based zombies."

I scoffed. "Right ... Can we presume it's an alias?"

Pearson smiled. "I believe we can make that perfectly reasonable assumption."

Minniva leaned over from her chair in the dining room. She made certain to look at me when she noted, "By the way, Detective? The demon doesn't like you."

I looked away from Pearson and back to the dining room. I smiled at her, trying to be reassuring. "I get that reaction a lot."

She actually smiled. "I figured that much." She paused, then furrowed her brow. "But can you explain why a demon would be interested in Rikers Island?"

My smile fell, and my heart sped up. My breathing became shallow. The scars on my chest tightened, almost like I was being speared once more with the ripped off prison bars.

Aw Hell—

Before I could say anything, I took a deep breath... only I was hit with the scent of evil. Then a thump hit the ground so hard that there were ripples on the water in a glass on the counter.

Speak of the Devil. "Kill all of the lights and get the guns. Something is coming."

11 / THE ESSEX HORROR

THEY CAME AT EIGHT IN THE EVENING.

Down the clearing, the property ended in a tree line, broken by a road up to the house. Half a mile down the road was a large 16-wheeler and several cars. They pulled to a park. But four black SUVs kept driving up the road.

I stood at the front door and looked out into the darkness. I drew my gun and placed it on the windowsill. Then I thought at the armor, calling it up to slide over me. The display focused on the men in the cars. It penetrated the glamour quickly this time.

The "private security types" were more serpent men. They pulled up to the house, swinging the cars around at right angles to provide makeshift cover.

I flipped two switches. I turned off the light on the porch and turned on all of the landscaping lights. Sinead had a lot of landscape lights, so the incoming goons were lit up like Christmas morning. The serpent men were in their black suit and tie, carrying automatic weapons.

But there was nothing out there that could have shaken the house. Not even the truck was close enough to vibrate the house.

The minute that I lit up the thugs on the front lawn, everyone else lit them up as well. Sinead, Alex, Mariel, Jeremy, and Pearson had taken up positions upstairs with rifles and opened fire. The first two to fall were felled with headshots—Jeremy and Alex, who both preferred right between the eyes. One was double-tapped in the head with the rifle, courtesy of Alex. Sinead and Mariel both put three rounds in their targets. Father Pearson fired six rounds so fast it sounded like automatic fire and put two rounds into the heads of his targets.

And this is why Mariel brings the guns everywhere now.

Each of the Serpent men gushed green ooze and faltered. The ones who had been shot in the head fell back and stayed down. Their bodies melted before they hit the ground.

The ones who had been shot in the chest, however, tottered and managed to raise their guns.

I picked up my own firearm and swung it out to fire into the surviving thugs.

The display on the helmet generated crosshairs that lined up with my gun sights. I snapped off several shots in short order, delivering the coup de grace to the wounded.

Oppose, O LORD, those who oppose me; war upon those who make war upon me—oh Heck!

More of the Serpent men circled around the black SUV. Most of them dropped as soon as they emerged, taking fire from above. But one of them drew down on me and fired.

The ethereal blue fireball that came out punched through the front door, slammed into my armor, and hurled me into the wall.

The armor display flashed red. A harsh warning beep pinged at me.

I touched the part of my armor where I had been shot... and touched my own chest. Part of the armor had been blown away. The armor grew back to compensate, but I had to keep my head down until it finished.

Take up the shield and buckler; rise up in my defense ... though I guess you did that just this minute.

Suddenly, the gun slammed back, hitting the serpent man in the face. The muzzle jammed under its chin and fired, cleanly removing the head.

Brandish lance and battle-ax against my pursuers... though I guess you just did that too. I need to pray faster.

I pulled myself out of the wall and looked over my shoulder. There was Lena. Her brows furrowed, concentrating on the enemy.

Lena had taken the Serpent's gun and used it against him.

She mentally grabbed his weapon and pulled it towards us. I caught it out of the air and glanced at it. It looked like a standard Thompson submachine-gun, only without the classic barrel-drum magazine.

I swung the weapon around and fired for one of the SUVs. It punched a hole right through one side and out the other. Serpent men scattered out from under the SUV, right into the welcoming arms of gunfire from the second floor.

Say to my soul, "I am your salvation."

"Are we shooting the turkeys, Hussar?" Lena asked me with girlish enthusiasm.

I smiled as I fired again, this time disintegrating a Serpent. "I think so."

Then, from a half-mile down the road, one of the cars around the truck was knocked away, sending the car into the air like a child's toy. *That's not good.*

Let those who seek my life be put to shame and disgrace.

With everyone keeping the Serpents down, I focused on what was coming. The armor's display zoomed in on the area. Nothing was there... except for the vaguest shimmer of "something." I could make out the faint outline of something big. Even the armor took a moment to piece together what was there. It was like the distortion of a cloaking field, bending the light around a *thing*. The thing was about fifty feet tall and thirty feet wide. It only vaguely resembled a thick human shape—like a Middle Earth Dwarf who grew or a Gumby who abused steroids.

With each step a new divot appeared in the ground like an oak tree stomping around.

We can target you, sucker, I thought before I went back to the Psalms. *Let those who plot evil against me be turned back and confounded.*

I raised the gun to my shoulder, took aim, and pulled the trigger.

The trigger simply *clicked.* The gun was empty. I frowned and put it aside, then swept up my sidearm. I aimed for the shape and fired six times, hoping to at least make a dent in it.

All six bullet strikes sparked against the air in front of it.

Then a roar shook the air. *I think I just pissed it off.*

I backed away from the front door and called up the stairs. "Alex, go mix us some Molotov cocktails!"

Lena knocked on my armored leg like it was a door. "Can I help, Hussar?"

I glanced her way. "You have any ideas?"

Lena looked out the door. With a glance, the SUVs all rolled at once, crushing the gunmen outside. Those that dove out of the way were exposed and shot. The slaughter was over in a matter of seconds. The SUVs continued to roll, until they blocked the exit at the tree line.

Make them like chaff before the wind, with the angel of the LORD driving them on, I prayed with a smile.

There was a growl, and the SUVs were kicked out of the way.

Lena's eyes narrowed. She was not amused. The footsteps continued to shake the house. Upstairs redirected their fire and started unloading into the space where the creature was.

Then Lena got annoyed. The SUVs lifted up from the ground and slammed into the creature. Small rocks flew up from the ground at it. Then small boulders. The trees uprooted and fired at it like a missile.

The thing kept coming.

Make their way slippery and dark, with the angel of the LORD pursuing them.

Alex tapped me on the shoulder with his elbow. He had two bottles in his hand with rags in the mouths. "Where do you want them?"

Lena looked at the edges of the rags, squinted, and the rags ignited. Alex jumped back and dropped both bottles reflexively. But they only dropped a few inches before they stopped in mid-air, then flew out through the front door screen and into the creature. It immediately caught on fire, covered in a blanket of flames.

But it didn't stop, and it didn't slow down.

Alex, still gasping for breath from the shock of Lena's little show, said, "At least, we can see it better."

I nodded. "Just great. Everyone, get ready to run."

Lena and Alex looked at me. "Run where?" Alex asked. "That thing is between us and the road out of here."

I lifted my fist with the Soul Ring on it. The armor had, as usual, made a gap just for the ring. "I'm going to keep it busy."

Lena clung to me like I wasn't going to come back. "Don't go."

I ruffled her hair. "Don't worry. I've literally got the armor of God."

I gently nudged her away and stepped outside. I circled right so the thing on fire could follow me—and so everyone could circle left if they needed the escape route. It wheeled around to follow me along my trajectory,

"Hey, dumbass!" I called out. "Have you come for me?"

The growl turned into a roar, and it charged.

I charged it, too.

Without cause they set their snare for me; without cause they dug a pit for me.

It leaped for me, bounding up at least thirty feet in the air, arm cocked backwards to pound me into Jello.

Let ruin overtake them unawares.

I shot forward and dove underneath it, then rolled.

The fist came down, missing me by yards. But the ground rippled in a shock wave that knocked me off of my feet. It turned around.

Let the snare they have set catch them.

Then it laughed.

My eyes narrowed, and I raised my fist. *Let them fall into the pit they have dug.*

"No more Mister Nice Guy."

I raised the fist, pointing the ring at the invisible beast. *Then I will rejoice in the LORD, exult in God's salvation!*

The jewel in the ring glowed white and fired a beam of light into the creature, punching a hole straight through the shoulder.

My very bones shall say, O LORD, who is like you? Who rescues the afflicted from the powerful, the afflicted and needy from the despoiler?

The ring fired again, punching a second hole through the monster. It staggered back. It let out a groan that sounded like the metal body of the *Titanic* hitting the iceberg.

Malicious witnesses rise up, accuse me of things I do not know. The ring fired again, ripping out a chunk of the creature's hip. It tottered, dropping to one knee and both arms. *They repay me evil for good; my soul is desolate.*

Yet I, when they were ill, put on sackcloth, afflicted myself with fasting, sobbed my prayers upon my bosom. The ring put another blast in the creature's head, knocking it to one side. It growled and tried to pull itself forward, limping forward to come for me.

I stood my ground, ring before me. *I went about in grief as for my brother.* It took a blast to the chest, and it reared back. *Bent in mourning as for my mother.* Another blast to the chest knocked it back on its haunches. "*Yet when I stumbled they gathered with glee, gathered against me and I did not know it. They slandered me without ceasing; without respect they mocked me, gnashed their teeth against me.*"

The Soul Ring glowed bright enough to turn night into day and launched a full blast into the beast. It struck center mass and punched into the main body, and exploded, blasting the upper half of the creature in two. It landed on the ground with a splatter, like fish guts spilling out.

I blinked. *I didn't even get to the end of the Psalm. Thank you.*

The creature melted away before my eyes, seeping into the dirt below. I didn't want to see what the grass around it would look like in a year.

I scanned the area with my armor and my own eyes. There were no other threats. I armored down, and said a quick *Thank you, God.*

I walked back into the house. My wife was on the porch, rifle in hand. She smiled sweetly at me as I came up the stairs. "Hey, you."

I smiled back and kissed her on the lips. "Hey."

I looked through the door into the house at Lena. She hugged Jeremy, happy the threat was over.

Mariel gave a happy sigh. "Lena's going to be a handful, isn't she?"

I gave a chuckle. "Let's hope there aren't too many bullies when she goes to school."

Mariel rolled her eyes. "Heck with that. I've been home-schooling Jeremy since we went into WitSec. I think we'll stay with it a while."

MINNIVA ATWOOD STILL SAT AT THE DINING ROOM TABLE. HER eyes were wide and startled. She hadn't moved since the attack started.

I winced. I had figured that she would at least know enough to keep her head down during the fracas. Apparently, so did everyone else. We had been so focused on our well-oiled machinery of shooting back, we had forgotten that she was essentially a civilian.

My partners were a cop and a former spy. Sinead and my wife and son were easy backup. My adopted daughter was a one-girl wrecking crew. That I couldn't even see any of us as civilians was problematic.

Pearson was right by her side, trying to soothe her frayed nerves. She had only been exorcised a few minutes ago. Since then, her world had been expanded from "black mass" and "demons" to a ring that looked like magic, powered armor that might well be magic, a twelve-year-old boy who provided fire support, and a thirteen-year-old girl who could kill people with her mind. All of which were used to fight "private security" mooks who survived three rounds to the chest, as well as an invisible mini-Kaiju that survived being hit with rocks and SUVs and being set on fire.

She'd had a tough day.

"Who the hell are you people?" Minniva asked.

I sighed, and I gestured to everyone to gather at the table. It was time to have a discussion that was probably long overdue. "You guys hold on a second. I want to check on Grace."

I charged up the stairs and went into our bedroom, where our daughter had a crib waiting for her.

She had slept through the entire shootout.

She's used to the sound of gunfire already? That's interesting.

I went down stairs, Grace asleep in my arms. I figured having the big burly man with the badge, gun, magic ring and magic helmet cuddling the perfect little bundle of joy would probably make Minniva feel safer.

The moment he saw me on the stairs, Alex said from the table, "Okay, Tommy. Now that you've gathered us all together, what exactly do you want to do?"

I sat down at the opposite end of the round table from Minniva. "My name is Detective Thomas Nolan. For lack of a better term, I am a..."

I didn't want to use the usual slang.

"Thaumaturge," Pearson filled in. "like a candidate for heaven who isn't quite there yet but asks god for help... and gets answered prayers. Some people call that a saint."

"But I'm not dead yet," I added.

I went back to the beginning, and everyone who had been at my side through every supernatural event was there to chime in and fill in the blanks. I started with Anthony Young and my first charism—bi-location into a clothes-line. I discussed how I could smell the evil coming off of a possessed criminal named Hayes. Alex could testify to our investigation of Christopher Curran, who had been the next person possessed by the same demons who had possessed Hayes.

Then we talked about the prison riot of Rikers Island.

Minniva's eyes opened as she stared at me. "Rikers Island. That's why they hate you?"

I shrugged. "Wait. We've barely started."

We went into the "Women's Health Corps," which was a death cult that took all of the body parts from their day job to offer up as human sacrifice to Moloch. But the cult was partially a payment system for a warlock in the mayor's office. We discussed how there had been a Dark Web bounty put out on my head by the warlock. That bounty had summoned Hell Hounds and scryers and vampires to come and get me. After the warlock had been put down, I had been transferred to "intelligence abroad" for the NYPD, connected to the Vatican.

We went into the complete story of the Soul Stone—a story that Alex Packard and Sinead Holland hadn't heard yet. It was a story about how two British Atheists named Fowler and Toynbee had conspired to use an ancient artifact to level London, Indiana Jones style. Fowler and Toynbee had allied themselves with a collection of Jihadis who had other plans in motion. The Jihadis had been led by an Imam Kozbar, who also had a sex slave network operating on the European continent. That led to a succubus named Jayden who tried to raise an army of demons in the name of Moloch. However, we had an army of golems made by the Rabbi of Prague and his son's construction company, as well as the Soul Ring, a chip off the old Soul Stone. So that sorted out the mess. Lena had been held prisoner by the slavery ring, which is where I found her.

Grace woke up part of the way through Germany.

Alex pointed at Pearson. "This was supposed to be a vacation until this guy showed up."

Pearson shrugged. "Sorry."

Alex sighed and leaned back in his seat. "Whatever. Hell, as long as we don't have to deal with the bokor again."

I winced. I didn't say anything about Bokor Baracus. Telling Alex that the dark Voodoo necromancer was still alive, despite everything that Alex had done to him, was not a conversation I wanted to have.

"And while he was gone," Alex continued. "I had a little fun with a coven." He smiled at Sinead. "Didn't we?"

Sinead rolled her eyes. "Let's pretend that never happened, okay?"

Minniva looked around the table. "No wonder you weren't impressed by everything that happened today."

I smiled at Grace and touched my nose to hers. "No, we aren't. Who's afraid of the big bad demons? Not us. Not us."

Alex sighed and shook his head. "Dang. Just when I think that it couldn't get any stranger around here, you guys think of something."

Pearson frowned. "Tell us a bit about Matchett?"

Minniva shrugged. "No idea. I know he's European. He's Jewish, if that helps."

Mariel cocked her head. "Odd last name."

Minniva blinked, then thought it over. "I think he changed it? Growing up? He's originally German."

Mariel rose next to me and took Grace. "Okay, I think we've done enough storytelling now. Minniva, after I put Grace to bed, Sinead and I can find and make up a place for you tonight. Father Pearson?"

He smiled. "I don't even know if we're done for the night."

"What else are you going to do?" Mariel asked. "Visit the VP for HR?"

Sinead looked up from her smartphone. She held it up so we could clearly see the results from the most useful investigative search tools in the world—DuckDuckGo. "There is no such person as a VP HR Herbert West in the entire state. If he owns property under that name, it's unlisted."

Alex snapped his fingers. "That's right. The *Reanimator* movies."

Everyone looked at him like he had broken out into word salad. "Herbert West? *Reanimator*? I think they were based on books?"

Mariel ignored Alex and looked at me. "You know I was joking, right? Do you really want to confront something else after dark?"

I looked at Pearson and Alex and shrugged. "Does anyone think that we can get the real address for VP West by talking to someone at Matchett Industrial when they open up in the morning?"

Alex scoffed. "If they did, I'd assume it was a trap."

Pearson frowned, then nodded. "I'd agree with Detective Packard. The only way to get any reliable data from the company might be to go in through the back door. Is there any way to break in?"

I shrugged. "I don't know. I think I can think of at least two ways to get in." I looked at Jeremy. He had nodded off during the story-telling somewhere in the middle of Germany. His arm cradled his head. "He can probably think of at least one, even in his sleep."

Without lifting his head or opening his eyes, Jeremy muttered, "Levitate up to the office and go in through the window. Bilocate into the office. Or use the power armor to scale the side of the building." He settled into his arms and went back to sleep.

I shrugged and looked at Pearson. "Told you."

Alex sighed and shook his head. "Kids and their superhero movies. In my day, we had to actually read the comics. And they were comics, not 'graphic novels.'"

I STOOD IN THE CORNER OF CEO GEORGE MATCHETT'S OFFICE, looking around the creepy room. It was a large corner office that could have doubled as a conference room with the right furniture. The lights were motion-sensitive, turning on when I moved. But the light didn't illuminate the edges of the room. The corners were so dark that it was like the lights weren't even on. The office was so high there was no lighting from the street—no street lights, no illumination from other buildings or signs. The moonlight from outside was deeply muted. I looked out. The moon was visible, but it didn't really add to the lighting.

To my complete lack of surprise, the room smelled like death, Hell, sin, and plain evil. My solution was the cotton ball–holy water filters up my nose once more.

The main desk was up against the massive windows. It was a large right-angle desk. The windows behind the desk made for the last two sides of a box. In the center of the room sat enough furniture for a living room. It had two black leather couches around a large coffee table. Two plush armchairs closed the box on either side.

One of the walls in the office was nothing but books. The bookcases went from floor to extremely high ceiling and wall-to-wall. It caught my attention. Instead of going to the main desk and the main computer, I went over to the bookshelves.

The first thing I noticed was that there were a *lot* of old books. Many of them were in German. One of the books was eerily more familiar than the rest. It was bigger than the average coffee table book and needed to be laid down on the side. The binding was black and in very wrinkled leather. The book had no title, and the cover looked like the wrinkles formed eyes and a wide mouth.

I described the book to Father Pearson as he sat on the couch back at the house. He cringed. "*Necronomicon*. Grimoire. It's bound in human leather. Don't touch it. Don't look at it too long. Don't even *breathe* too close to it."

I backpedaled and sidestepped, moving away from the evil book. I started looking at the others, and read them to Pearson. He sat back in his seat and closed his eyes. He searched his memory as I read the titles. Half of the time, I struggled with the German.

With every title, Pearson winced. His face became darker and darker. He took Alex's glass of scotch and took a healthy sip. "Grimoire. *Book of Shadows*. Oh gawd, *Sixth* and *Seventh Books of Moses*! Pseudo-Hebraic mystical symbols, spirit conjurations, and founded Rastafarians. Probably because you have to be high to believe it."

I cringed and read another book. "The ... *The Clavicule of Solomon*. Did they mean the collar bone?"

Pearson groaned. "Probably the first grimoire on record."

"*Petit Albert*."

"Enlightenment magic textbook," Pearson explained. "Don't even ask about the Hand of Glory. Keep going."

I stumbled over an entire shelf of German, then tripped over trying to pronounce them. Pearson sighed and shook his head. "Just stop. I think you've stumbled upon the first editions of the Nazi occult section of the library."

"How can you tell they're first editions?" I asked him.

Pearson rolled his eyes as he slammed his head against the back of the couch. "Because every attempt to make a second edition drove the copier insane or destroyed the copy machine."

"Ah, good reason."

A quick skittering sounded behind me. I whirled around, reaching for my handgun, but nothing was there. Nothing except for the shadows.

Because those are just so comforting.

I stared into the darkness, waiting for something to stare back. When I finally detected some movement, I couldn't tell if the shadows were actually moving or if I had just stared at it too long.

Time to make this a rush job. Our Father...

I continued praying as I darted over to the computer. I booted it up, and the lights flickered. The computer asked me for a thumbprint. I looked over at the print reader and smiled. I sprinkled a little holy salt on the print reader, then gently blew it off. The oils from previous fingerprints had not been wiped away. I pressed down with a sheet of white paper, and the scanner acknowledged the fingerprint. I was in.

The lights in the office flickered again. The room dimmed. I typed faster. The first thing I did was call up the address for Herbert West, VP HR. The file didn't even give us his photo. But it had his home address and his other contact information, and that was enough.

I shut down the folders on screen and was close to shutting down the computer and getting out of there.

The sound of big, booming footsteps suddenly filled the hallway. I reached for my gun and took a step back, ready to draw down and open fire.

My foot came down, and something *crunched* underneath.

I looked down. I had stepped on a cockroach. But there were five more nearly on my heel.

I nearly bolted forward into the computer.

On the main screen was an open folder that had already been open before I turned on the computer. It was named "Recent Documents."

"Cold Spring Harbor?" I read aloud.

Back at the ranch, safe in the dining room, Pearson said, "American Eugenics program, mid-20s, I believe. Not quite Nazi-level bad, but they were all horrific. Why?"

A rat darted through the dimming light in the main room, coming straight for me. Roaches crawled onto my shoe and worked their way up the desk.

"It's a file on the computer," I told him as I clicked it open. More rats appeared from the shadows and skittered my way. The footsteps in the hallway *boomed* closer.

I wished I had my armor on as I continued praying. The Cold Spring Harbor file was a list of donations. Some were projects to Watson, of DNA fame, as he worked on his own, updated eugenics projects. There were a score of them.

A roach crawled onto my hand as I scrolled further. I flicked my wrist and pounded my fist down onto the bug. Six more jumped for my hand, and I pulled it away.

Rats crawled onto the front of the desk. One leaped for me. I batted it away with my free hand. Bugs crawled up my pants leg. I slammed it up against the desk to crush them, but I kept reading through the list.

The *booms* came closer, rocking the door.

Nearer the bottom of the list, my eyes locked on in disgust and repulsion. "Donations—the Women's Health Corps Nationwide and Mayor Ricardo Hoynes."

Back home, Alex groaned. "Seriously? Why is it always a Demoncrat donor?"

A rat jumped for me. I punched it out of the air and sent it into another rodent. They fell into a fight among themselves. That didn't matter, a dozen more closing in. The bugs bit me. I swept down the inside of my leg, crushing them all.

The fighting rats rolled over the keyboard. The file skipped to a most recent donation.

"More recently. There is also a substantial endowment to a Professor Noah Whateley of Dunwich University."

Pearson grunted. "He makes Peter Singer look like Mother Theresa."

Alex said, "Who?"

I ignored them both. "All of these donations? Prompted by the VP of HR. West."

Another rat jumped for me. I backed away from the computer, stepping on more roaches. The rat landed on my shirt. I grabbed it by the neck and hurled it across the room.

Time to leave.

The door burst open. Furniture between the door and the desk went flying. Something unseen slammed into me, slashing at my chest, ripping into my flesh and rending bone. I slammed up against the windows as the rats and the bugs had unfettered access to me as the blood flowed.

I screamed as I was eaten alive.

13 / THE DREAMS IN THE SUMMER HOUSE

It was not the first time that I had technically cheated death by bilocation. I say technically because every time I had been more than one place at a time, the double died. I ended up with inexplicable scars that would eventually confuse the funeral home director that processed my body. The scars on my hands, feet, and sides only looked like stigmata. But like the holes in my chest, they had been remnants of previous deaths of my doubles. And while I had felt every moment of my previous deaths, and retain almost perfect recall of the agony, I could usually tune out the pain of one death in my other-self.

This time, no such luck.

And unfortunately, as with the Soul Ring, the golem armor had not come with me when I bilocated.

I screamed in pain as I fell off the couch in Sinead's living room. Alex and Pearson came to my side as I writhed on the floor. I flailed and kicked out uncontrollably. It was like a seizure combined with being on the rack. Pearson and Alex grabbed my arms and pinned me down. I kicked out, breaking the leg on the coffee table.

My roars of pain shook the house so much, Sinead, Mariel, Minniva, and the kids all came down. The two women grabbed my left leg, Lena reached out with her mind and pinned down the other. Jeremy hopped onto my right leg like he was helping.

After ten minutes of screaming agony, I mercifully passed out.

As I went limp, everyone looked at Alex and Pearson. Mariel's mouth was a tight line of tension. "We were gone five minutes. What the—" She glanced to Jeremy and Lena, and said, "heck happened?"

Jeremy coughed politely. "I think you mean 'Hell,' Mom. It's only accurate."

Mariel opened her mouth to scold him. She paused, thought better of it, then glared at my two partners.

Pearson held his hands up as if to say *don't shoot*. "He thought he would give bilocation a spin. He figured that if that didn't work from here, then we'd have to plan out a raid on Matchett Industries with levitation or the armor. Levitation would need tools, and smashing through with the armor would need timing. Tommy thought that if he could sit on the couch and pray, if God wanted, then He would allow Tommy to bilocate straight into George Matchett's office."

Mariel pointed to my motionless form as Sinead took my pulse. "Then what happened?"

Alex shrugged. "No idea. He said something about roaches and rats, then ... this."

Sinead frowned at the sight of blood coming out my nose. "How about he not do this again," she stated.

Mariel leaned over and knocked on my chest. "What about the armor? Why didn't he use it?"

Pearson shrugged. "Neither the armor nor his ring bilocate with him. It seems that it's one of the few things that ability cannot duplicate."

Mariel's eyes narrowed. "A simple breaking and entering, and it still turns into a nightmare."

I groaned as I awoke and tried to move. The most motion I could make was to lift my arm a few inches, and my index finger after that. Mariel was at my side, grabbing my hand. "Tommy, are you okay?"

I cracked one eye open. "I plead..." I took a deep breath. "The fifth."

Mariel laughed reflexively. "What happened?"

I tried to shift so I could get more comfortable, but I felt like I had gone through all five beaches of Normandy on D-Day. Every part of my body felt like I had been beaten with a metal bat. "Rats. Bugs. Eaten alive. It sucked." I paused to focus on breathing. It hurt. "And something else. I didn't see it, but I felt it. All over."

I tried to squeeze Mariel's hand. It was a feeble effort, but she felt it.

"Back up a second," I said.

She placed my hand on my chest. I thought at my golem armor. The sheets of clay slid out from the chest piece, down my arms and legs. I skipped the helmet. The animating power of God flowed through the armor and into me. It absorbed a lot of my pain. Strangely enough, that made it ache more. But I breathed better. After a moment, I used it to get into a sitting position.

I groaned. "Ugh. That sucked."

Minniva looked at me, then at everyone else. "How many times has this happened?"

Mariel sighed as she cupped my cheek with her hand. "I've lost count."

I thought over the last moments before everything turned to pain. I looked at Pearson. "You said something about a professor? Dunwich University?"

Pearson nodded. "Professor Noah Whateley," he answered. "Makes Peter Singer look like Mother Theresa, is I believe what I said."

Minniva frowned. "Who's Singer?"

Pearson closed his eyes, took a deep breath, and let it out slowly. "Bioethics professor over at Princeton University. Probably evidence that evolution is reversible. Singer's entire deal is the right to life is tied to pain and pleasure. Abortion is perfectly fine, since 'they're not rational or self-aware.' Thus under that rationale, they can hold no preferences. The baby can't object. Therefore, a mother's preference to have an abortion automatically takes precedence."

Minniva's face went through several iterations as she processed this. Her brow furrowed, and her mouth bunched up in thought. "Okay? I guess?" She shrugged. "It doesn't sound any different from any other argument."

Pearson held his hands up, acknowledging that. He didn't argue any position of the faith but moved forward. "Singer also applies this to newborn babies. 'Killing a newborn baby is never equivalent to killing a person.' And he has clarified that even if life *does* begin at conception, that isn't 'sufficient to show that it is wrong to kill it.' "

Minniva's mouth dropped, and she raised a hand, about to speak. She paused, then shook her head. "Listen. I am a glorified sales rep. I don't know much outside my field. But, um, doesn't that sound like an argument used by every other ethnic cleanser?"

I tried not to laugh at her phrase. "Ethnic cleanser" made it sounds like taking bleach to a family tree. Maybe something to mix with amniotic fluid *in utero* to make certain that there were no genetic defects.

Pearson nodded. "Oh yes. He's all for infanticide. He's all for euthanasia–I think he even coined the term *non-voluntary* euthanasia."

Minniva was speechless. Her hand came up and waved around, as though she were in the middle of a rant, but nothing came out. "What? *Non-voluntary?* Tell me that's not actually something a real human being has said after 1945." She pointed at Pearson and his Roman collar. "You. Don't you have a phrase for this? Sanctity of life or something? Doesn't all that go against ... this?"

Pearson smiled, almost a laugh. "Oh, Singer agrees. He thinks it's outdated, unscientific, and irrelevant. He says he's far more interested in elevating animals, not lowering humans. We won't go into Holocaust Surviver and Nazi Hunter Simon Wiesenthal's opinion of him. Though he was fairly nice about it.

"But despite all of that, Singer took care of his aging mother until the very end. She had Alzheimer's. He could never explain why. Not even to himself." Pearson rolled his eyes. "Because apparently, he didn't even consider that caring for your parents is a naturally-occurring process. But that would require he consider a natural law that wasn't pure pain/pleasure."

Minniva grimaced. "And what about this Noah Whateley guy?"

"Oh, he thinks that you can kill any offspring up to age ten without any consequences since no child is really rational until then. Maybe the harshest penalty is like for the first offense at animal cruelty. At the other end, he insists that anyone over the age of 75 has a *duty* to die. If they don't exercise that duty themselves, then it should be inflicted upon them. After all, they would eat up Medicare after a while. If you have cancer of a certain stage, insurance shouldn't be obliged to pay for it, nor should anyone else. He's for ethnic preferences in terms of medical care–triage should be less about who is most likely to be saved and more about the color of people's skin. Since white people have more privilege, their obligation is to die whenever possible. The fewer people there are, the more resources there are. It's very much recycled Malthus and Ehrlich, only with more Gaia and environmentalism thrown in."

Minniva, the head of sales, just stared blankly as Father Pearson threw in more names she didn't know. The priest sighed and said, "He thinks that the villain Thanos is the real hero of the Marvel movies."

"Oh."

––––––––

THE NIGHTMARES THAT EVENING WEREN'T STRICTLY nightmares. They were more like flashbacks.

Every minute of my sleep was an endless stream of my deaths. Not the painless moments of bloodless death in Rikers, where an artery had been nicked during a firefight. No. It was the painful, horrific ones. All of them. The impalement on bars ripped from concrete. Twice. Being beaten to death by an angry mob with cricket bats. Being burned alive with Molotov cocktails as the fire slid down my throat like a snake made of napalm. Or when the shadows of London came alive and speared my hands and sides, reeled me in and ate me alive.

And, of course, last night. The bugs. The rats. The thing in the dark.

All of those incidents were comparatively quick the first time. Unlike the original deaths, these nightmares moved painstakingly slow. First time through, these had been over in seconds–at most, minutes. Each death in my dream allowed me to appreciate every second. Each individual spear to my chest felt like a separate and particular instance. Instead of a quick spear of darkness, they were slow drills. I felt each bite of bug and rat.

No matter how many times I had been killed in action, I had always walked it off. In part because my deaths, though vivid and real, had always been quick. Had I been awake for this experience, I'm certain one theory would be PTSD catching up with me.

But during my sleep, I had *known*, for a *fact*, that I had woken up in Hell.

I woke up with a start at 5:30 in the morning as my alarm went off. I shot straight up and scrambled to put my back against the headboard. I looked around for the nightmares waiting for me. My breath came quick and pulsing, like I was in the middle of a speed record while lifting weights.

Mariel was already awake and watching me. Her eyes were wide and startled. "Tommy. You're bleeding."

I looked down. Blood covered my side and my arms. Only some of it got on the sheets. I brought my hands up to my face. I saw right through the holes in the palms. The scars had opened up and turned into holes that punched right through my hands.

I winced, but flexed my fingers. There was no pain. I reached for and ripped off the blanket to check. The scar in my side had also opened up. The same with my feet.

The door burst open, and Lena charged into the room. She looked around for a threat, then locked onto us. "Hussar. Are you okay?"

I held my hands up with a smile. "Don't shoot. Nothing ... all that wrong. I think."

Lena smiled. "Stigmata! Yay!"

I winced internally this time. I was not interested in showing off ... anything, really. Stigmata was usually empathy with the Crucifixion taken to such a degree that the wounds of the Crucifixion manifested on the one doing the meditating. It was the sort of thing that appeared on someone who would become a saint.

My first thought was how to cover it up.

Don't get me wrong, even at the time I knew that it was an honor. God wouldn't allow such a thing to happen unless He thought I was deserving.

However, one of the few things I prided myself on was that I *didn't* shove my faith into other people's faces. Yes, I was at every church function that didn't drive me insane, but I was support. I was background. One of my biggest takeaways from the bible was Jesus' suggestion that one should avoid praying in public on street corners but to go pray in a closet. (You'd think the closet would be extreme, but during the time of Jesus, it may have been the only way to get even a modicum of privacy within one's own home.) While I didn't go pray in a closet, I tended to keep my rosary out of sight, or otherwise spend my time trying to blend into the background.

Displaying stigmata? It wasn't quite the exact opposite.

There was another problem I had to consider—the amount of fights I got into. Making a fist would at least put one finger in the wound. I didn't know if there was concern about lint in stigmatic wounds.

"I'm going to need some bandages. And gloves." I smiled at Lena. "You think you can manage that?"

Lena nodded eagerly and ran off.

I swung my legs out of bed and bit back a groan. Trying to move made me feel like I was still in the body that had been dismembered last night. My joints and muscles hurt.

I said a quick *Our Father* as I willed the Soul Ring to kick in and heal any wounds in my arms (not my hands, I wasn't going to spit that in God's face). It didn't work. It only took me a second to realize why it didn't work–I wasn't actually hurt. I didn't know if the pain was spiritual or psychological, and I didn't want to ask too closely.

"Did you sleep well?" Mariel asked. "You were thrashing in your sleep."

"Bad dreams," I told her as honestly as I could.

Mariel let out a breath. "Whew. Well, not surprising, considering what you've been through."

I smiled as reassuringly as I could. "Probably."

As Lena came in, and she and Mariel worked on bandaging me up, I dwelled on my night of horrors. Only one solution came to me: demonic assault. I'd had the experience only once before, and that sucked. It seemed whatever we faced had had enough and had sent up a flare for help. And Hell obliged.

After they finished wrapping up my hands and feet, I thanked them and told them I was going to church.

Lena patted me on the leg. "I will go with you."

"You don't have to–"

She waved away my objections like I was talking nonsense and ran off for her bedroom.

A QUICK VISIT TO MORNING MASS CLEARED UP MOST OF MY aches and pains. I had a coughing fit so hard that I had to leave mass for a few minutes. I coughed up three nails that dissolved on the pavement.

So I was cursed on top of that. Yay.

By the time mass ended, I easily able took communion. Since Lena and I were the only people on our side of the church, the two of us finished off the chalice.

As we walked out of the church, Lena patted me on the hand as though I were a lost puppy she had to console.

Breakfast was more like a war meeting.

The first topic was the priority. That was getting Minniva to safety.

Minniva wore a heather gray, short-sleeved light mock turtleneck that fit her more like a tunic, plus dark blue yoga pants obviously borrowed from Sinead. Her navy high top sneakers looked more like Jeremy's, but I wasn't going to ask. We weren't going to ask her to run around in the scarred Louboutins she'd arrived in. She twitched a little but seemed relatively calm. Mariel had opted for something more practical than yesterday. She wore black jeans and charcoal cotton shirt with rolled-up sleeves. Paired with old Blundstone steel-toed boots I hadn't seen in a while. Grace was loosely draped in a cotton blanket while sporting a Tardis blue "Relax, I'm the Doctor" onesie Jeremy had picked up somewhere. Jeremy was, of course, wearing an Iron Man t-shirt and jeans. He gestured at the brassy image of an armored Tony Stark and gave me a thumbs-up to let me know he wore it in my honor. Sinead wore a cream-colored long-sleeved tee and dark slim jeans, plus her ever-present Israeli army boots.

Sinead shrugged. "I have no problem with driving her out of the area. A few hours in the car should get her away somewhere safe."

Mariel frowned as she held Grace. "I don't like you two going out by yourselves. You'll be a moving target. I think you should have more backup." She tilted the chair back from the dining room table. "Though on the other hand, I'm not sure how we'd mix and match."

I winced at her predicament. If we didn't have a newborn, I would have suggested that Jeremy go with all of the ladies into one car. That way there would be enough firepower in one car.

Then again, there was a way of doubling the firepower with Sinead as well as maintaining manpower in the house.

"Lena, would you mind going with Doctor Holland and Miss Atwood?"

Lena looked up from her breakfast, delicately trying not to get anything on her pink dress. She nodded eagerly. "Of course, Hussar. I hope that they come for us. I want to see what happens when I blow out tires at nearly a hundred kilometers an hour!"

Jeremy grinned. "That would be so *cool*." The two children high-fived.

Alex casually sipped his coffee. "I think the kid's gonna fit in perfectly around here." Alex was in his usual cop casual uniform of khaki pants and golf shirt, this time a green and white number from the Connecticut branch of the National Association of Fire Investigators. I turned my mind away from speculating on how he managed to acquire it.

"Once we're done getting Minniva to safety, I think we should go to the beach," Mariel said casually, trying to deflect from the violence of children.

Pearson merely rolled his eyes over his mug of tea. "And what about our day's objective? Hmm? Mister Herbert West?"

I shrugged. "Actually, I thought we could swing by Dunwich University. Last night made me curious what a guy like Matchett could get out of donating so much money to a college professor involved in bioethics."

Pearson frowned distastefully. "Wasn't last night more than enough? Do you really want to know more about the man?"

I smiled. "Think of it this way. It'll be some intelligence gathering. And we're going to need as much intelligence as possible when it comes down to it. West will be an interrogation. Possibly a firefight and an interrogation with pliers. Whateley will just be reconnaissance."

Alex and Pearson both looked at me like I was insane. Alex replied, "Did you just say 'how hard could it be?' I'll go get my chemicals."

I rolled my eyes. "Father Pearson, what's the word on the package from Rome?"

He checked his phone. "I got a message at three this morning. It's en route. And it's a nine-hour flight from Rome."

"Noon then. Good. We have time to kill."

DUNWICH UNIVERSITY WAS A PLEASANT LITTLE CAMPUS. THE buildings were all made of stone, and relatively short. Some of the smaller buildings were modified homes and cottages. They had their own little stone chapel with a small graveyard in the back. While paths lead throughout the campus, everything else was grass. Most of the paths weren't wide enough for five people to walk shoulder-to-shoulder down the walkway.

There were only a handful of students actually out and about. They seemed standard for late teenagers and early adults. Some sat on wooden benches, chatting amicably with books in their lap. Others wandered the campus, backpacks fully loaded and heavy with books. There were even the usual smattering of students with their smartphones out, staring blankly into them, as though the phones were smarter than they were.

And every so often, there would be a shirt, or a flier hung up on a tree or a bulletin board, that referred to the university as "Old Miss" or even "Old Missy."

How do you give a University a nickname like "Old Missy" from "Dunwich"?

"What do you figure?" Alex asked. "A hundred students?"

Pearson shook his head. "No. Not quite. I'm thinking more along the lines of two or three hundred. You'd be surprised how many people you can fit onto a campus. Especially if you have night classes."

I said nothing as the two of them continued to bicker over the campus population. It was one of those places that felt comfortable to a city dweller like me, but laid back enough to be considered almost a vacation. It wasn't anything like Oxford, but it felt similar. It was, externally, peaceful.

For no reason I could give, the campus felt ... off. There was no smell of evil. There were no strange sounds, unless one thought that the breeze was odd.

It took a moment for me to realize that the armor was giving me a tingling sensation.

Okay, okay, I thought. *I know. Something's wrong here. We figure out what, and we can proceed.*

The building for the bioethics department was another house. It was a nice home. It was two stories, with a lot of windows, with metal siding, painted yellow.

Pearson knocked first.

After a minute, a man in a smoking jacket appeared at the front door. He had just barely entered middle age. He was a big man. He had four inches on me in height, and about a foot in width. His forehead was so broad, it nearly looked like he was balding. His hair was a light brown, or a dirty blond. It was a little long, only a few inches from being tied together in a ponytail. His facial hair was somewhere between "five o'clock shadow" and "goatee."

"You seem a little old to be students," he said.

"We're not," Alex told him. He flashed his badge so fast, no one could have read that he was from the NYPD. "And you are?"

He smiled easily. His hands in his pockets, he seemed calm. "Professor Noah Whateley. Chair of bioethics for Old Miss."

Whateley seemed unconcerned with our presence. If two cops and a priest showed up on my doorstep, I would assume that Alex had died when I wasn't looking and had been shot in the line of duty. If I were a civilian, what would be the first thing to come to mind?

Pearson nodded. "We're doing a little bit of research on one of your benefactors. A Mister George Matchett?"

Whateley shrugged. He didn't even bat an eye. In fact, he glanced at me and smiled a little. He knew something I didn't, and he enjoyed the secret. "Yeah. Sure. I know him."

"What we were wondering is what could he have contributed to?" Alex asked. "Matchett himself doesn't seem to be very much in the biotech industries."

Professor Whateley glanced at me again as he answered. I hadn't even asked him a question yet, so what could he have possibly found so interesting about me?

"George Matchett simply approves of my *philosophy* in bioethics." He turned his gaze to Father Pearson. "You may have heard of some of my positions on the chaff in our society?" He waved his hand dismissively, as though banishing refuse to the outer darkness. "The under-ten and the over-seventy crowd can *easily* go. It's not a terribly uncommon thought within our society, but most people seem to stop there. *Yes*, these people are *parasites* on society. *Yes*, they contribute nothing while consuming many of the goods and services we use. Ask any new parent what the cost of a child is like. Ask anyone with overweight and senile parents what it's like when they fall down, and the caretakers need a derrick to pick them up off the floor. However, no one seems to wonder, why only restrict this by age? It's only natural that's what we should be thinking."

My partner arched a brow. "And what is your final ... solution?"

If Whateley picked up on the comment, he didn't note it. "Stop all vaccinations and increase the level of undocumented aliens into the country."

I blinked and exchanged a glance with my partner. Alex shrugged.

"That seems very ... specific, Professor."

Whateley shrugged. "Oh, they *have* to be undocumented, Detective Nolan. The undocumented are poor. They've dealt with most of the exotic viruses out in the world without the aid of modern medicine. They are stronger. Tougher. More resilient by the experience. White people? Pfft. White people are too soft in comparison."

Wait, what did he call me?

Alex nodded slowly, the sort of thing he would do when talking with a homeless EDP— emotionally disturbed person. "So what did Matchett want you to *do* with the money, exactly?"

Whateley smiled slyly, as though he were doing the easiest thing in the world, and we were far too stupid to do the same thing. "From Old Miss, I lobby politicians. With a few phone calls, I'm involved in distribution. The strategic placement of the undocumented in areas where they can leave the most impact."

Pearson arched a brow and said, dryly, "You mean infect the most people?"

Whateley spread his arms and grinned. "Exactly!"

At that point, I realized that he called me by my name and rank, even though I hadn't given him either. I summoned my armor with my will and forced it to slowly unfold down my arms and legs, staying inside my clothing, but giving me protection.

"Evolution in action!" Whateley continued excitedly, ignoring all of our reactions. "We cut out the soft from humanity, and promote the stronger. The superior! After all, the people we want in our society are going to be good communists who can work together. They will be sane, rational people who know that God is dead—or Islam! Which knows that God is merely a good tool in the hands of the state." He looked at me, and he winked. "The better to tax the infidel into next week."

My armor flared to life and armored me up all the way. With a push of my legs, I leaped into Professor Whateley shoulder first and drove him back into his porch. We crashed into the house, smashing into a table in the front foyer. I slammed Whateley into the wall so hard he left a hole in it.

Normally, I wouldn't use the armor against a civilian, but it was clear that this wasn't a civilian. If he had been, I would have broken ribs, bruised his spine, and otherwise nearly killed Professor Noah Whateley.

Whateley grabbed me by both shoulders and threw me away, still in my armor. I came to my feet as Whateley rose, unconcerned and smiling.

"What gave me away?" he asked.

He shot in and backhanded me in the helmet. The clay buckled and dented, and the impact sent me into the wall, leaving a bigger hole next to the one he had left.

"Your name?" Whateley mused. He nodded to himself. "That was it, wasn't it? I should have opened with it." He punched into my gut, doubling me over. He didn't leave lasting damage, but too many hits like that, and I didn't expect my armor to hold.

Whateley threw his hands up in an overly dramatic shrug, then led it into another backhand. "I should have opened with it. That I recognized the smug, sanctimonious cop from New York City. 'Of course, detective, you made national news when you took down that

serial killer and quelled a riot.' Or maybe the WHC. Or the mayor."
He kicked me deeper into the wall, driving me in like a nail. "Pity
you're too stupid to live, *Saint*."

The door closed behind Whateley. It slammed in the faces of
Pearson and Alex without any human hands going near it. It locked
itself.

Whateley slid his hands back into the pockets of his jacket.

I was still lodged in the wall but on my feet. I reached around
with my left hand, searching for something to grasp. A bit of elec-
trical cable would do. Some piping would have been even better.

I spared Whateley a glance. "Have we met?"

Whateley grinned. "Oh, the whole hosts of Hell know who you
are, Detective."

The display in my armor showed me an aura around Whateley. It
shimmered in black and red. The walls no longer looked solid in my
vision but more like Jello, as though the house was made of
ectoplasm.

Hmm. With my left side, pinned into the wall, I punched up
through the guts of the house.

The house roared in agony.

Whateley looked around, concerned at the noises the house
made.

I ripped my fist out through the wall and swung for Whateley's
face. His head barely flinched with the punch, and I had been able to
punch through concrete with this armor.

My second punch was an uppercut to Whateley's belly. The
impact lifted him off the floor.

Whateley backhanded me and sent me flying for the side wall of
the porch and a new gaping hole in it. This new hole was a gaping
bottomless chasm—

And this hole in the wall had teeth, with a six-foot gaping maw.

Why does the bloody wall have teeth?

I slapped the floor to stop my momentum. The wall warped and
twisted and snapped at me with razor-sharp fangs. I pushed away, to

my feet and twisted around so my back-fist smashed into Whateley's face. I sent him sprawling.

I threw myself into and through the front door.

The whole house growled behind me. The growl was like a bear the size of a bus.

"*Run!*"

15 / THE DOOM THAT CAME TO
       DUNWICH U

I took six bounding steps down the path, then stopped dead, surprised by the sight of the campus through the display of my armor.

It was a sight of the Dunwich University campus without the glamour used to conceal the truth.

While the path was unchanged, everything else was turned into a warped nightmare. Each building had teeth in the mouth of each doorway. The windows flickered like dozens of eyes. The students that carried their books as anyone would—some in their hands, some wore backpacks...

All of them were in various states of decay.

The ones carrying books and talking to each other only had the beginnings of decay in the side of the faces and arms, black veins running down nearly to their hands. The ones with book bags had the corrosion running up and down their bodies, with dead, vacant expressions.

The ones on smartphones, though, were dead inside and out. Empty eyes, flesh missing out of their cheeks so I could see their teeth, or flesh hanging off their fingers or around their eyes.

Others were different. They seemed to be alive and lively, with scales covering parts of their flesh. Like scales that hadn't been fully shed from a fish, or maybe the slow formation of a cocoon, ready to change the students into something ... Other.

The security guards were the most familiar things—they were Serpent men constructs.

The lawn rippled as though it was alive.

I flung my arms up to stop Pearson and Packard from running past me into a dead student.

"Necromancy," I said aloud.

"Damn it," Pearson spat. "Old Missy! I missed the connection. Bloody Lovecraft!"

I watched as the students poured out of the buildings. A handful of security guards closed in on us. They didn't have to rush. The paths were narrow, and the big, burly men sauntered casually towards us. But behind them, the crowds of students filled in the space. The Serpent men security guards were only there to slow us down while the students formed a barricade.

Pearson moved back to back with me, and Alex fell into the formation. His gun was in his left hand, one of his metal saint cards was in the other.

Alex kept an eye on the incoming. "What do you mean, Lovecraft?"

"We're in Essex County. It's where his city of Arkham and Miskatonic University were located."

Alex growled. "He made up Arkham and Miskatonic U! THEY WERE FICTION!"

"No, he changed the names to protect the guilty. Why do you think they call it Old Missy?"

I had a sudden thought back to the end of my mission in Germany. The terrorists had summoned and bound the demon Asmodeus. I didn't want to hear anything he had to say. Even if it was the truth, it would probably only be a detriment for me to know. As I walked away from him, he screamed that what was coming was something that H.P. Lovecraft would have approved of.

I guess he was right.

"Why are they only blocking the paths?" Alex asked as the students and Serpent men security guards closed in on us.

"The lawn is ... rippling. I think it's also alive."

"The lawn is lava. Got it."

Whateley slammed into me from behind. I stumbled forward three steps, then spun and bent in half, hurling him to the path. I stomped for his head. Whateley rolled out of the way and onto his feet. He leaped for me, and I burst forward, blocking his right round-house and drove into his gut with a left. Both strikes felt like hitting stone.

I swung my right fist up into his face and brought my left down into a liver shot. He might have been unhurt by the blows, but his body mechanics knocked his head back, then doubled him over.

This meant I could easily grab him by the skull. I planted my right foot just past his left side, then twisted my body around, hurling Whateley into the great lawn. He bounced and rolled with each impact as he came to a stop in the middle of the yard.

The lawn instantly rippled to life around him. The surface was more like water in the middle of the tide coming in.

Whateley stood in the middle of the lawn, raised his hands to the sky, and laughed.

The Serpent guards and the students stopped a few yards away. There was nowhere for us to go, so why bother? The only path not blocked led us back to the horror house behind.

Whateley called out to us, "Did you think that you could defeat me by feeding me to the campus? The campus is our focus. It is a source of power! I control it! We are unstoppable."

Whateley reached down like he was gathering sand in his hand, even though it was still at waist height. Ephemeral eldritch energies pulled up from the lawn, turning into a ball of gold and purple plasma that swirled and danced like a beach ball of lightning in his hands.

"Brace!" I called.

Whateley threw the ball. Lightning shot out from it on all sides as it rushed towards us. Another blue flame ignited at the core as it shot down.

It came down with the speed of lightning.

But the Soul Ring reacted at the speed of thought.

A shield of pure white light appeared in front of me. The purple plasma struck it and exploded. The bright blue fireball was immense and consumed all it touched. It blew out parts of the path and dug a hole in the dirt several yards deep and wide. Lightning crackled from it, striking the nearest conducting surface—the Serpent guards. Blue lightning shot out to the sky, turning the clouds black for a moment before it shot back down and struck the great lawn. The buildings howled. The trees screamed. The lawn writhed in agony and rippled as far away from the damage as it could.

When the violet flames cleared away, it left scorched earth like glass. The campus had been so badly wounded, the abomination within had been cauterized, and the sickness purged.

I and my partners, however, were left totally unscathed. The shield conjured by the Soul Ring had been perfect, and had reflected everything sent at us.

Whateley glowered at me. "Okay," he said flatly. "No more Mister Nice Demon."

He pointed at me. His finger lit up from the inside. The same eldritch energies as before gathered at his back, a capacitor with a full charge.

I raised my fist with the Soul Ring pointed at him. It glowed white, ready to do battle with damnation.

I smiled behind my helmet. "Bring it, bitch."

The laser shot out and struck my shield. I was content to let him waste his ammunition. I figured out why we had come. If the university was a focus, a source of power, then it was something built up over years. There was nothing in my arsenal that could contend with that power out in the field, especially if I didn't know where or when it would turn up. But here, at the source of that power, I had a chance.

I thought at the Ring my intentions. And it wasn't just for salvation from the dead. The serpents and the students both closed in.

O God, you are my God—it is you I seek!

The shield became like an umbrella over us, coming up and dropping to the path in a curtain of light.

For you my body yearns; for you my soul thirsts, in a land parched, lifeless, and without water.

The shield expanded from us in an ever-spreading ball of light, pushing back on the death beam from Whateley. It pushed out from the path and struck the lawn.

I look to you in the sanctuary to see your power and glory.

The lawn rippled and thrashed against the shield, but it gave way and calmed. It became smooth and quiet. It flattened out like a rug being smoothed out against heavy furniture.

For your love is better than life; my lips shall ever praise you!

The Serpent guards held their weapons at the ready, bracing against the might of God's light. They leaned into the wave of the shield's energy, and the white light consumed them, only leaving ashes behind.

I will bless you as long as I live; I will lift up my hands, calling on your name.

The curtain of light washed over the student body. Many of them looked frozen as the light poured over them. But when the light moved past, students staggered through and wondered what was going on, unaware of what happened.

My soul shall be sated as with choice food, with joyous lips my mouth shall praise you!

The students who looked dead and rotted under my display were hit with the light and seized up, then they dropped like a switch that had been hit. They had been dead already. The light merely purged the dark forces that had been animating them.

I think of you upon my bed, I remember you through the watches of the night You indeed are my savior, and in the shadow of your wings I shout for joy.

The ones dead inside, but not decaying, fell to their knees and wept.

My soul clings fast to you; your right hand upholds me.

I turned my attention, and the attention of the ring, to the rest of the campus.

But those who seek my life will come to ruin; they shall go down to the depths of the netherworld!

The light of the ring smacked the house behind us. It roared and bellowed like it was being vivisected. The house itself leaned into the light to fight, and it fell back, stiffening as the eldritch horrors were purged from it.

Those who would hand over my life to the sword shall become the prey of jackals!

The lawn rippled under Whateley, dragging him back, away from the curtain. He gathered up the energies left around him and made a motion to push off the ground.

It sent him flying away.

But the king shall rejoice in God; all who swear by the Lord shall exult, but the mouths of liars will be shut!

The curtain of light blew through the rest of the campus, flushing out the rest of the satanic energy. The buildings became normal. The lawn settled and became as Earth. The students, however, freaked out, especially at the dead friends and fellow students fallen at their feet.

Then, the curtain of light disbanded, falling away. As soon as the light from the Soul Ring cut out, so did everything from it. I armored down before anyone really paid attention to me. It was bad enough that the students had gone through trauma from Hell.

But Whateley had gotten away.

I narrowed my eyes and looked off into the distance with my display. Whateley was already out of range.

"What the heck was that?" Alex snapped. He turned away from the once-hostile mob and back to me. "Was that you, Tommy?"

I shrugged and raised my fist with the ring. "It was this."

Pearson frowned, bending his beard. His brow furrowed harder than I had ever seen him. "Interesting. I'm almost surprised that Whateley, whatever he is, didn't allow you to escape and continue the pursuit off-campus. If the campus was a source of power, the first instinct wasn't for him to drive you off of it." Pearson waved at everything that had been cleansed of the dark powers. "Why even risk this? Why announce the power here? Why make it a target in this way?"

I was about to answer that evil tended to overreach so hard they dislocated something, but that struck me as wrong. Something big was coming. It had to be. It was the only way any of the forces of darkness would consider risking themselves. They had been concerned about the monks Minniva had contacted, so they had to be stopped before the monks turned it into a race against time. They bought themselves at least a day and a half – Pearson took time to cross the Atlantic, and it took us time to track down Minniva.

But something big was coming, and the campus *was not a part of it.*

But if the campus isn't part of it, I thought, *then what was it for...?* *Excess resources. Backup.*

"A trap," I said aloud.

Alex and Pearson looked at me. Alex cocked his head. "You mean it was meant to lure us in and kill us?" He scoffed. "Obviously, that worked so well."

I shook my head. "Last night, we took out whatever horror they sent after us. But we needed the ring." I pointed my fist at the stretch of lawn where the flames had turned it to glass. I said a quick *Hail Mary* to activate the ring and heal the land.

The ring flickered and fixed a square foot patch.

I raised my fist to Pearson's eye level. "They wanted me to burn through the power of the Soul Ring. They had to know I had something like it—if the forces of Hell talk to each other, the Succubus from Germany would have told her bosses. They would have told Whateley and everyone else involved. They wanted me to burn through the power in the ring. And now we're down a weapon."

I grimaced. "Come on, guys. We're going to visit VP Herbert West of Matchett Industries. And we're going to kick down his door and ask him some questions."

The three of us cut along the yard to the parking lot. We were in the car and moving in a matter of minutes. Pearson was on the phone to the Vatican, informing his boss of the situation at Dunwich University. Alex checked his magazine load out and patted himself down as though he had forgotten a weapon.

I focused on the road ahead and paid no attention to anything in my way.

I was pissed.

I was angry because they had held an entire campus full of student hostage to dark forces. If I hadn't come along, they would have all probably been thrown into Hell or sacrificed, or possessed for the rest of their life, spreading misery and living in Hell on Earth.

I was angry because they had decided to use my compassion for others as a way to "disarm" me and the ring.

I was angry because God is not mocked. And that was Whateley's day job.

My drive through Massachusetts was a blur. I was so aggressive, even local drivers got out of my way.

I pulled up to the address at eleven o'clock in the morning. I opened the door before I turned off the engine. I swung outside and hopped over the hood of the car. I armored up before I even reached the stairs, and I kicked the door in. I didn't even bother drawing my gun. I felt like hitting something, and I hoped that I was going to find a supernatural idiot ready to attack me.

I found "Vice President for Human Resources Herbert West" standing in his living room. He wore a raincoat long enough to cover a multitude of sins. He was tall, long and lanky. His was a bald

Haitian with long, spider-like fingers and a huge, wide grin. He spread his spindly arms wide in greeting.

"Detective!" he cried out in his lyrical accent. "I'm so glad you found me! I was just trying to look up your number, but no one seems to know it down in New York anymore."

Alex charged in right next to me. He cursed and drew his gun. "Damn it! Not again!"

Pearson jogged up next to Alex. He looked to "Herbert West," then back to Alex. "Sorry, haven't had the pleasure."

"Officially," he said, "I am VP for HR Herbert West."

I finished for him. "He's really a Voodoo necromancer named Bokor Baracus."

I ARMORED DOWN MY HELMET BUT LEFT THE REST OF THE armor active. I didn't want to get caught flat-footed by Bokor Baracus. Never again. He had tried to kill me more often than I could count and had been at least partially responsible for every single time something supernatural had tried to kill me. Even if he wasn't directly involved, he had played a major supporting role that had enabled the threat to happen in the first place. He was a mystical mercenary. As part of keeping himself alive against all odds, Baracus was obligated to help his fellow demon-worshipers. In Germany, they had made the mistake of "letting the check bounce"—a phrase I didn't want to inquire too closely into.

Alex had his gun level with Baracus' head but reached for another saint card. "What the Hell is he talking about, Tommy? Why would he try to call you?"

Baracus smiled at Alex, as though he were late to the conversation. "As I have told your partner once before, Detective Packard, I am a mercenary. I work for the side of evil because they pay better. However, the last thing I want is for an actual end to the conflict of good and evil. Hell wins, I have earned pride of place … in Hell. Oh, yay. Heaven wins? Hell keeps me forever. And they do not reward failure, no matter how many years of loyal service one has given."

Alex paused for a moment, frowned, shrugged, and glanced at me. "It makes sense. After a fashion."

I nodded slowly. I was tempted to reach for my gun or test the Soul Ring and its charge. "And what of your current employers?"

Baracus spit on his floor—a nice Persian carpet, so Baracus was not happy. "Bah! I have recently begun to believe that the scope of my consultation with Mister Matchett is somewhat *wider* than I have *contractually* agreed to."

Alex blinked hard, confused by the legalese, and even more thrown by Baracus using it.

Packard: "What the hell...?"

Baracus gave a deep, long-suffering sigh. "I believe that Matchett is going to go full Gozer. He may even be trying to prompt the End of Days."

Father Pearson arched a brow. "Funny. I don't recall a CEO being mentioned in Revelations."

Baracus cocked his head at the priest, as though wondering if he was truly serious. "Matchett needs a legion of demons. Can you imagine something *else* he would need it for?"

Alex's eyes narrowed and snarked, "How about to take over New York City?"

Baracus looked like he was going to reciprocate the snark but paused and shook his head. "No. While I understand what you mean, Matchett is old. He is dying. I see it in his frail form daily. His aura fades. He did not exchange his soul for more *life* but for *power*."

Pearson circled around to the right. He wanted to be in a flanking position if he needed to be. "Unlike you?"

Baracus gave a rich, deep belly laugh and bowed. "*Guilty*, me lord. I am an impatient man who desires to live until the stars go cold. I may even get to a confessional first if the inclination strikes me." His smile faded. "But Matchett desires to fulfill his master's wishes before the end. Perhaps he thinks to find a more exalted place in Hell."

I raised my own brows. While Baracus had turned on his German employers for a bounced check, all he had done back then was offer me a location—Germany. This sounded more like he was offering direct help. "Won't *your* Friends on the Other Side dislike you turning on Matchett like this?"

Baracus' eyes narrowed. "He didn't tell me all of his plans. This means that he is in violation of our contract. Hell takes its contract violations seriously. We have the lawyers to prove it. Though we are allowed to enforce our own violations. Hell is big on the self-made men. They tend to worship their creators."

I nodded to the large armchair in the center of the living room. "How about you sit down, and you tell us what exactly you *have* done?"

Baracus gave a Gallic shrug and threw himself into his chair. "Where shall I begin?"

"How did they contact you?"

Baracus smiled broadly. "All rich people know each other, Detective. At least, many do. They are a small network of people. If you were to guess, what would you say?"

I winced, not liking the implications. "Matchett gave to the Women's Health Corps."

Alex scoffed and rolled his eyes. "Dear God, them again. What did they do? Loan you out for a weekend? Then you got a permanent job with him after New York fell apart?"

Baracus' smile this time was more subdued and tight-lipped. "How droll, Detective Packard. However, there was more of a gap than that. Matchett needed a book or two to add to his collection." Baracus looked at me a moment and studied me. His smile lengthened a little. "I was told that someone broke into Matchett's office last night. I was also told that the intruder was dismembered, disembowled, and devoured. That wouldn't happen to have been you, would it, Detective Nolan?"

My voice stayed flat and neutral. "I was there."

He nodded deeply, happy to be correct. "Then you saw his

collection of books. The library is quite extensive. After New York ... fell apart, as Detective Packard puts it, I needed another employer to support my lifestyle. So Matchett put me in touch with friends of his. More wealthy people. More self-made men."

I sighed deeply. I had so wanted to never hear their names again. "Toynbee and Fowler, in London. That's how they consulted you on the Soul Stone."

Packard held up a hand. "Hold on. You were *there*, too? Is there anything in the world you're not attached to?"

Baracus glanced at me, amused. "You did not tell him that I was alive? Such an oversight. I feel slighted."

I shrugged. "I wanted Alex to sleep at night."

Alex opened his mouth and paused. He thought about how long ago London had been, figured out that the knowledge of Baracus being alive would have cost him nearly six months' sleep, and let out a puff of air. "Yeah. You're right. It would have sucked."

Well, that went better than expected.

Baracus smirked, then shrugged. He apparently thought the same thing. "I went to the Fowlers, worked for them. Kozbar had me work on a side job Germany... then his check bounced. I suppose he should be fortunate that you got to him first. But after London, I came back here and worked for Matchett. He wanted demons. He wanted possession. He wanted his entire company possessed. He has a power base at Dunwich University."

Alex laughed. "He *had* a power base at the university. Tommy got it."

Baracus blinked. He looked at my face, then my armor, then locked onto my ring. He cocked his head to the side like a velociraptor eyeing prey. "Ah. You have a part of the Soul Stone. That's good. It will be useful in the battles ahead. I ..." He drifted off, squinting at the ring. "Purging the university emptied it out, hasn't it?" He leaned back in his chair, steepled his fingers, and growled in frustration. "Now I know why they wanted a place of power independent of the possessions and the black mass."

"You've done your job," Pearson said. "Why not leave?"

Baracus shrugged. "Matchett wanted me to stay. Be on retainer. It was little enough. And the money was right. At worst, I think he wanted me around to ride herd on the possessed and make sure they didn't get out of hand."

That sounded right. "One thing. You said you were going to try to call me. What prompted the call? You've been here for months. You performed the black mass months ago. What made you want to contact me now?"

The bokor sighed and wiped his brow, even though I didn't see any sweat there. I hadn't thought before then he had a nervous habit. "It is a long and complicated process. And while I casually stated that there could only be one purpose for the demons, I may have exaggerated. A little." He looked around. No one believed him, but we wanted him to keep going. "When you know as much as I do, there is a list of things that Matchett could do with this many possessed. But time has passed. Months have passed. Certain things need certain conditions to happen before they can be executed. Many of them have passed. An equinox. A solstice. There are very few things left. Unless it is something I cannot even begin to imagine. And I have an excellent imagination, detective."

I narrowed my eyes, trying to see to his heart. *Then again, I presume he has one. Bad mistake.* "But I ask again. Why *today?*"

The bokor raised his eyebrows and spread his hands in a welcoming gesture. "Because, Detective! They have let the entire company have the day off. Across the entire country. Everyone has been told to stay home. Including security. So whatever they want to do, they want to do it today."

I had several thoughts at once.

If they shut down the company, all of the possessed will be free to roam. They may not even gather at the building.

Why would they gather at the building? They might as well be a hive mind.

If there's no security, we can break in.

We can destroy the books.

– but there's no security, and I broke in last night. Would they have really left the library there intact?

Which means it's probably at Matchett's house.

They're going to pull the trigger on their plan today. Maybe even right now. The end of the world could have started, and my family is out there driving in it.

But who knows what's going on? Matchett.

Who can tell us how to stop it? Matchett.

I turned to Bokor Baracus. "Okay. Fine. Let's play. What do we have to do to find out what's going on? You must need us for something. Otherwise, you would have done it yourself."

Say Matchett. Say Matchett so I know I can trust you to the next step.

"Why, to George Matchett's house, of course. He's the only one who would know everything. Unless you can interrogate a demon."

I turned to Father Pearson. "What about the package?"

Baracus and Packard turned toward me.

"Package?" Baracus asked.

Packard frowned. "What package?"

I smiled. "Wouldn't you like to know? Father?"

Pearson smiled sheepishly. "I only got a text about it a little while ago. The plane was late. It didn't take off until about six o'clock in the morning, our time."

I narrowed my eyes. "And you said it was a nine-hour flight. I hope the apocalypse can wait until three in the afternoon."

EVERY ESTATE IN AN AGATHA CHRISTIE STORY, EXCEPT FOR THE occasional quirk relevant to the plot, was essentially the same. Each mansion was more like a castle. They all had reading rooms, libraries, foyers, parlors, game rooms, a den, and several wings. The estate grounds were wide and luxurious, spanning acres. The hedges were all neatly-shaped, and the lawns neatly mowed.

George Matchett, however, had lawn care HP Lovecraft would have loved. Vines overgrew the bushes and fell out of them in tangles like tentacles. The vines even overgrew the front wall and the massive iron fence at the front gate. The sculpted bushes on the lawn were not cute cuddly animals or artistically pretty objects—they were hideous creatures from beneath the sea. The most normal-looking animals were lobsters, crabs, and starfish. Some of the others looked like warped, mutated sea creatures with claws and fangs. Others still looked like deformed plant versions of the Serpent men I'd fought for the last 24 hours.

Then there was a rhino thrown in there – possibly because the plant sculptors had run out of ideas.

The walkways between the lawns were cracked and broken. The

driveway came in through a side gate in the wall, up to the front door, then back into the garage.

The security was, of course, what you would expect from a multi-billionaire. There was an arsenal on site. The guns they owned were banned by Massachusetts state law, but Matchett had paid his way around the laws. His guards hadn't come into conflict with the law often, since the estate signs warned away all trespassers as far as the road. The few times anyone had come out here were decades ago, when one or two girlfriends of the billionaire had gotten their hands on a phone and dialed 9-1-1, crying for help. When the police arrived, there were supposedly no girlfriends and no phone call. Later, a girl from the nearest city would be reported as a "runaway," complete with a neat, typed note to the family.

Ten guards in teams of two patrolled the front of the house. There were twenty guards on each side of the house, also patrolling in twos. They were armed with MP-5 sub-machine guns. Mister Matchett, of course, was all in support of gun control. Obviously, in this case, that meant that his guards hit what they aimed for.

Thankfully, in the back of the house, there were only two guards. Most people would be forgiven for thinking this was a shocking over-sight. However, the back yard terminated in a five-hundred-foot drop into the ocean at high tide and jagged rocks at low tide. WiFi cameras had been placed all over the mountainside in order to alert the guards to any climbers. They rotated back and forth, more than enough time to catch anyone as they climbed.

However, we weren't going to climb.

During his time working with George Matchett, Bokor Baracus had been allowed to borrow the company boat. It comfortably fit six ... or uncomfortably sat a priest, two cops, and a bokor.

As we approached the house around noon, clouds had gathered in. The day was still pleasant, but deeply gray and overcast. It felt like a day to go to the beach. It didn't look like a day to go out of the house if you looked at the sky. The meteorologists at Google, Yahoo, Brave,

DuckDuckGo and the Weather channel all agreed that the day was going to be sunny, and all of the clouds were going to burn off.

However, as the water churned and the seas shook the boat to and fro, we didn't quite believe it. The winds had stayed at "easy breeze."

We parked the boat as close to the edge of the water as we could. The next part was all on me. More specifically, on God. There was only one way we could get up there fast enough to avoid the cameras, and it wasn't by my free-form rock climbing in armor.

I armored up, and Pearson handed me the grappling hook. The best plan we had was for me to levitate straight up with the three of them already on the rope. I would pull them all up behind me, hook the grapnel in the cliff's edge, then tangle with the guards while they climbed the rest of the way.

The only prayer I could think of for the occasion was to Saint Joseph of Cupertino, the levitating patron saint of pilots. After all, it worked when I had jumped out of a tower before it exploded.

I closed my eyes, held fast to the rope, and prayed.

Dear ecstatic Conventual Saint who patiently bore calumnies, your secret was Christ the crucified Savior. Who said: "When I will be lifted up, I will draw all people to myself." You were always spiritually lifted up. Give aviators courage and protection and may they always keep in mind your greatly uplifting example.

Amen.

I opened my eyes and found myself already up in the air, climbing rapidly to the cliffs.

Then I disappeared into the mists.

Mists? There weren't any mists down below.

The mists covered everything, even though there was no logical reason for them to be there. A quick check on the sensors of the armor told me that the mist terminated at the border of the property.

Magical mists. Great.

The display shifted on the helmet to allow me to see what I was doing.

The cliff edge was right in front of me.

I raised the grappling hook over my head and brought it down into the cliff like it was a hammer. It drove the hook all the way into the dirt and left its mark.

I kept levitating, this time into the face of a guard. The Serpent guard blinked in shock as I landed in front of him. I punched into his face with the armored fist, grabbed his head, and hurled him over my shoulder off the cliff. His screams blended perfectly into the crashing waves below.

The next Serpent guard I saw hadn't seen me through the mists, but I found him. I made it to him within two bounds, coming down on him from above, making certain to stomp on his head with the full weight of the golem armor.

A quick scan showed me that two guards were all there were. I headed back to pick up the others. Mist made it hard to see where we were going, but I led the way. My armor helmet display pierced the mists and allowed me to guide everyone to the rear of the house.

Once we got to the backyard, Baracus led the way. He had visited the house before and had made a point of surveying the building. Apparently, it wasn't a response to something Matchett had done, but something Baracus did with every employer. As he put it, "I only needed one murder attempt by a client who refused to pay me to make that a habit."

We went in through the kitchen. There was no staff. There were no butlers or cooks. There were no maids. Most importantly, there were no guards. The house itself was in total disarray. Books were strewn about everywhere. Few surfaces were dust-free. Layers of dust were not the exception, but the rule.

Alex looked at me and smirked. "Remember the old Chiclet factory? The particulate bomb?"

I winced. Growing up in New York, there was a part of Queens near the 59th Street Bridge—commonly known in popular fiction for killing off one of Spider-Man's girlfriends—called Long Island City. It was a heavily industrial area. In November of 1976, there was an explosion that had blown out all of the windows, wounded 55 people and killed one. The entire explosion had been set off by a layer of dust over the factory floor and a single spark.

I nodded. "I'd be afraid to fire off my gun in here."

Alex paused in front of me, then turned around. "Give me a second." He ducked back into the kitchen. After a few seconds, he came back out. "Just setting something up ahead of time."

We followed Baracus through the dark, dusty house. I was tempted to try out one of the lights, but I didn't want to risk alerting the guards outside. We would have enough problems without that. I rarely had to interrogate a supernatural without them thinking they had the upper hand. When he was an enemy, the only way we had gotten Baracus to tell us what we needed was when he wanted to buy time for reinforcements to arrive. It was hard to imagine how Matchett would think he had the upper hand with four of us in the room, while he had one foot in the grave and the other on a banana peel.

The master bedroom was larger than my living room. It may have been bigger than the entire first floor of my house. Again, the first thing I thought of was Agatha Christie and the luxuriant homes of her murder victims. One had been murdered in a bedroom with so much furniture it had been stacked to the ceiling so it could come down in a crash to wake the house.

George Matchett's room was much like that.

The four-poster bed had curtains around it. The curtains were tied to the posts at the corners, so we saw Matchett clearly enough.

Packard sauntered in and sat on top of the cedar chest at the foot of his bed. I stood next to him. My armor was still up, and I was reluctant to put it down. While the glamour had hidden the sights and smells of Dunwich U from my senses, my armor had prevented me from smelling the campus after the illusion fell. I wasn't interested in finding out what fresh Hell scent this room had for me.

Pearson and Baracus took up positions on either side of Matchett.

The old man's eyes opened, and he smiled at us. "About time you made it here."

18 / THE LAST STATEMENT OF
GEORGE MATCHETT

GEORGE MATCHETT LOOKED LIKE HE HADN'T AGED WELL. While people had made jokes about Pope Benedict XVI looking like *Star Wars'* Emperor Palpatine (and from certain angles, I could see it), the former Pope looked better than Matchett at the same age. Matchett had had his hair replaced with younger hair plugs and dyed black. He was busy dying but that hadn't stopped him from dyeing. His thick, fleshy lips looked swollen, as though he had lost a fight.

Matchett's skin was the worst part. He had been a big, beefy man at one point. But he had lost all of his body fat. His skin now sagged, like a clown coat on a concentration camp survivor. Even if it hadn't, the skin looked like it was scarred and pitted. I had never seen leprosy, but if I had to guess, it would look like this.

Matchett looked to Baracus. "Have you betrayed me at last, mercenary?" he asked, his voice weak and thick with a German accent.

Baracus gave him an evil smile. "You should have told me all you wanted. Your secrecy has allowed me a free hand to act against you."

Matchett gave a wet, hacking cough. I half-expected blood. "Perhaps. But it doesn't matter." His shoulders twitched, and I could tell that he tried to shrug.

I leaned forward, pressing my hands on the trunk next to Packard. "Tell us what you did, Matchett."

Pearson stepped forward. His hands were clasped in front of him, and I could almost see him ready to give last rites. "We could consider it a confession, if you want."

Matchett gave a laugh that was barely distinguishable from the cough. "A confession? You have to be sorry to confess. And I'm *not*." He gave a smile that showed perfectly formed, fake teeth, stained with years of coffee and tobacco and whatever else he'd put in his mouth. "I regret *nothing*."

"Then what are you doing today?" I asked. Lightning cracked outside as God gave me a soundtrack to interrogate to.

Matchett looked decidedly unimpressed. "I am fulfilling my last payment to my master."

Packard growled and leaned forward. He had out one of the saint cards, rolling it in his fingers from one to the other. He managed to make it look like a rubber hose. Given what Matchett had been into, it might have had the same effect. "By doing *what?*"

"Paying my debts," he rumbled. "I was recruited by the Nazis when I was only ten years old, you know. They would ask me what or who had been hidden in and around the camps, or the ghettos."

Alex held up a finger, confused. "But you were Jewish."

Matchett coughed a laugh. "Bah. In name only. We were good secular Jews. We knew the state only had our best interests at heart." He gave a little smile. "When I could tell the guards and the SS what they needed, they would give me sweets." His eyes drifted and became glassy as he became caught up in 1940s nostalgia. "It had been the best time of my life. I had everything. My parents scolded me. Told me I was betraying everything they were. But my masters told me, and I knew better."

I tried to wrap my brain around a man who said it was the best time of his life just because the Nazis had indulged their young spy with all the treats they could come up with. He was a ninety-year-old man with the mentality of a spoiled child.

I couldn't even process it. Thankfully, I didn't need to understand his evil, just listen until he gave us what we could use.

Matchett's face became sterner for a moment, but his eyes hadn't focused on any one person. "But near the end of the war, I needed a new name. A new number. A number that did not mark me as one of them. So I made The Deal." Matchett's nostalgia grew into a dreamy smile, and he got caught up in his storytelling. "A deal for *power*. For *fame*. For all the money I could want or need."

Great. The prosperity gospel according to Satan. Here I thought Joel Osteen was bad enough.

Packard flicked the card back into his palm. He sighed, annoyed that he had to humor a 90-year-old Nazi out of some bad B-movie. "Big task," he stated flatly. "Can't imagine it had been easy on your end."

Matchett's eyes flicked to Packard and then drifted past him, over the shoulder. "Oh, it had been *easy*. Europe was a people broken. It was easy to push the agenda. Where had God been during the war? The Soviets had laid the groundwork in *Investia*, explaining how Pius XII had collaborated with the Nazis. They knew that secularism was the paving-stone road that would lead them to victory."

I was so tempted to snark that it was why John Paul II had helped destroy them, so their hostility had only led to their own destruction. But that would have interrupted the flow. So I settled for letting the plain, blank mask of clay hide my smile and mute my chuckle.

"From there, it was easy. Rights didn't come from God. They came from the state. If the states gave the people their rights, they could take them away. This upsets the people. When the people become upset, a few money transfers to the right people starts a war! Ha!" The dreamy smile came back. Who knew that reliving the havoc of wars and revolutions could be nostalgic? "But the real fruit has been harvested in the last few years. My lawyers have all but shut down Christmas. In a few years, no one will be able to hang Christmas lights in their front yard, lest they make atheists uncomfortable. I gave money to the right people to become priests and enter seminaries so they could filter out any with a sense of resolve." His eyes narrowed, sly and cunning. "The socialists have it right, you know, words have all the power. Redefining having a moral code as 'moral rigidity' has kept more people out of the seminary than the more ... heh ... unnatural appetites."

Pearson still had his hands clasped in front of him, but they had tightened. The knuckles became white with rage. The priest kept his hostility out of his voice. "You paid people to let pederasts into the priesthood and keep good men out?"

Matchett glanced at Pearson, then gave another cough and laugh at the same time. "Bah! Good men. No such thing. Goodness is just one maggot on a pile of shit yelling at another maggot. Both of them telling the other what's right or wrong." He frowned, a mocking scold. "And please. They are pedophiles. They merely love children? And who doesn't love children?" He cackled, his voice becoming slightly stronger. "It's just another lifestyle. Heh."

Packard cocked his head. "Nice," he pandered. "You promoted priests, and *they* became child molesters. But out in the secular realm, it was just another lifestyle. Impressive balancing act."

I made a mental note to compliment Pearson and Packard for falling into an easy good cop/bad cop routine.

Matchett smiled at Packard in a vague fashion. "Of course. Lawyers can do anything. And I have legions."

Baracus looked at us and shrugged. "This is true."

I blinked behind my helmet. I was almost surprised that Baracus had kept his cool during the interrogation and that this had been his first words since it began. Though in retrospect, I shouldn't have been surprised at the time. After all, Matchett and Baracus were more or less on the same side.

Packard ignored Baracus and said to Matchett, "I suppose the girlfriends weren't that impressed."

Matchett had a flicker of grin. "When they complained, I would add another wing to the mansion. They would go under the floorboards. Checks would go out to the right people, and the girls would have never existed. And I was Jewish. Any accusation was anti-Semitism." He gave another horrid, hacking laugh.

Packard nodded slowly. "And you were driven out of Germany?"

He rolled his eyes. "They call it currency manipulation. I call it good investments."

"I'm surprised you didn't move to Israel."

Matchett smiled. "That racist country? Never! Build a synagogue near Palestinians? How dare they! Make gardens and farms out of the desert? The desert is the culture of Islam!" he declared with a laugh. He seemed to get stronger the more he elaborated on his works, reveling in his cleverness. His eyes drifted around the room, not focusing on anyone or anything.

I had a sudden burst of panic and thought at the armor to throw up every sensory input it had in its arsenal to construct a warning map. A little circle appeared in the lower lever corner of my vision, like a sonar map. A blue dot was on my immediate left and at my 2 o'clock on the right—Alex and Pearson. At the outer edge were red dots moving around the circle. They were the guards on patrol outside.

Baracus was a purple dot on my 10 o'clock. Even the armor didn't want to classify him as a friendly.

Matchett was a stationary red dot right in front of me.

In my main screen were several levels of augmented reality. Translucent snakes ran all along Matchett's body. They were all latched onto him like leeches. A little label next to them classified them as minor demons, feeding on Matchett. I couldn't tell if they were killing him or keeping him alive.

"I'm surprised you decided to come here," Alex prompted Matchett.

Matchett tried that dying twitch again. "By then, my work had been done in Europe. I had kept God out of the EU. My brown shirts —who call themselves *anti*-fascists, can you believe that? My brown shirts rampage through the streets of Europe, smashing church statues and setting fire to cathedrals, all in the name of my master. I had hoped my good socialists—sorry, *anti-fascists*, heh—would do the same for America. But they never had the chance to take hold here they way they did in Europe." He paused, thinking for a moment. "Though I did convince Oregon to restrict insurance. Paying doctors to kill patients but not pay for heart transplants. Ah! *Der Furher* would have been *proud*. And getting all of the right people to accept the drugs I've helped legalize! Wonderful."

My patience wore thin with this old son of a bitch and his reminiscing. He wasted our time and did it deliberately.

The snakes fed on Matchett. They gave me an idea.

I raised my hand in the sign of the cross and blessed Matchett. My golem armor had caught my mood, and my voice came out like Darth Vader as I said, "I bless you in the name of the Father, and of the Son, and of the Holy Spirit."

The demon snakes on Matchett's body writhed. Matchett writhed in turn, screaming in agony. Bacarus backed away, as though he feared back-splash damage from the blessing.

Matchett settled down after a moment. I checked the sonar screen on my display. The red dots on patrol outside did not move or come to his aid. We still had time.

"What are you doing *today*?" I snapped, the voice modulation still in place.

Matchett looked at me and snarled, his face feral. "Damn you! Go to Hell, you—"

"You first, you monstrous son of Satan." I felt my adrenaline spike with my sudden rage. Listening to this vile serpent recite all his old vices had made my temper rise, and I hadn't even known or noticed until that moment. "*Our Father, who art in Heaven, Hallowed by They name—*"

Matchett screamed and gripped the bed as he thrashed. "No! No! I'll talk!"

"*Thy Kingdom Come! Thy will be done! On Earth, as it is in Heaven!*"

"Stop!" he cried again.

Even Alex knocked on my armor to get my attention. He patted the air in front of me, signaling me to take it down. I pointed at Matchett. "Start talking. When you're done telling us *everything* ..." I pointed at Pearson, "the priest will *stop* blessing you."

Pearson took the hint and reached inside his coat for his breviary.

Matchett's focus locked on me like a hungry squid, and he spoke as fast as his health would allow. "All I needed to do at the end was raise a demon incarnate. For that, I needed a host of the possessed to lead the rituals. I needed the right books. *All* of the right books. And in the end, the last thing was to choose the form of the destroyer."

Alex looked at me like he had fallen down a rabbit hole. He whispered, "I hope to God he doesn't say the Stay-Puft Marshmallow man."

Matchett sighed and groaned at the same time. "The best I could do for my masters was raise ... Tiamat." He gasped for breath as the demons increased their pace, feeding on his soul. Pearson thumbed through his breviary in front of Matchett. The old bastard kept talking, but this time, he gave one last smile. "And ... the ritual ... already ... started... an hour ago."

WITH THAT LAST STATEMENT, GEORGE MATCHETT GAVE A LAST gasp, then went limp. Pearson reached over to touch his throat. "He's dead."

The demon snakes stayed attached to Matchett, as though feeding on his corpse. They didn't move. I didn't know if they were going to stay there until removed or until his corpse rotted.

Before I could ask any follow-up questions about Matchett's last statement, the red dots in my sonar display stopped moving. "Guys. It's time to go. Now!"

Baracus again led the way. Pearson was right behind him. Alex was a little slower. He pulled out a cigarette and lit up before he got to the door. I brought up the rear. The red dots from outside closed in. The guards, at least, knew that Matchett was dead. He knew rambling at us would hold us here—either until the ceremony happened or until his death. If the former happened, we'd have lost. If the latter, then the guards would come straight for us.

As we raced into the outer hallway, the armor threw a flashing red icon on the right side of my display. It spelled out NATURAL GAS LEAK.

I thought back to Alex stepping back into the kitchen before we went upstairs. Then I looked at his lit cigarette. "Alex, what did you do?"

He looked back at me, lit cigarette in his mouth, and shot me a tight-lipped smile. Pearson caught the smell of gas and placed a handkerchief over his mouth. Baracus didn't seem fazed.

As we ran into the kitchen, the front door was kicked in with a bang. So were the doors on the side. They were all going to converge on the bedroom—they couldn't have known about us; otherwise some of them would have circled around to the back door to make certain we didn't leave that way.

Baracus and Pearson ran for the back door. The burners on the stovetop had been left open on high. They had been billowing gas the entire time we were in the house.

Alex slid over to a corner of the room and took a book of matches out of his pocket. He opened the matchbook and slid his cigarette into the book. He wrapped the cover over the cigarette and put it back in place. This locked the cigarette in place. He pushed the lit cigarette down the book, perilously close to the matches. "We may have a minute," Alex said. "Assuming they don't come shooting."

I winced. The lit cigarette and the matchbook was an old arsonist trick. The cigarette did not burn hot enough to ignite the gas. But the cigarette *was* hot enough to ignite the matches, and that flame would ignite the gas. The lit cigarette would burn down to the matches, and *boom*.

"When did you start thinking like this?" I asked.

Alex shrugged as he moved for the back door. "When you left for Europe. I don't have superpowers. I gotta think ahead."

Pearson waited for us at the door. When Baracus saw we caught up again, he strode out into the back lawn.

In my display, I saw the lawn ripple to life, as it did at Dunwich U.

"Baracus!" I called out, trying to catch his attention. I worried about alerting the guards in the house, but I didn't want to see Baracus eaten by whatever eldritch horrors awaited in the ground.

Baracus leaped off the grass and onto the pathway. Like at the campus, that seemed like a safe place to stand.

Except the vines that crawled along the lawn came to life and shot for Baracus, wrapping around his wrists and ankles like snakes shooting forth to strike.

Pearson raced for Baracus as he reached into his jacket. But more vines shot out, wrapping around the priest, and pinning his arms to his sides.

Alex spun around and flicked a metal saint card at a vine that lashed out for him. Like with the grapefruit trick with the playing cards, the metal card cut through the vine. It went still in mid-strike, then fell to the ground, just another plant.

Alex reached inside his jacket pocket and came out with a packet of red dust. He ripped off a strip of adhesive, exposing a metal strip of magnesium to the air. More importantly, it had been treated with something that ignited with oxygen. Alex threw it away, and it already ignited. The packet landed in the rippling lawn and burst open, spilling ignited thermite over the grass. The lawn rippled away from the damage, and several of the vines off of the house thrashed in pain, like a speared octopus.

I leaped for Pearson and grabbed the vine that held him. More vines shot out for me and wrapped around my upper body. I bent down and the vines around my upper body snapped like twigs. I grabbed the vine holding Pearson with both hands and pulled it apart, releasing him.

Alex raced for Baracus. The bokor fought against the vines. It was a standstill. He pulled against them, and they did not give. They pulled back, and he didn't move. But it took all of his strength to hold that tie. Having faced Baracus in hand-to-hand combat, he was strong enough that I was happy to be wearing my armor.

"Machete on my belt!" he told Alex.

Alex didn't even hesitate. He pulled the bokor's coat aside and grabbed the machete. He whirled on the vines and cut Baracus' hand free. Baracus reached over to free his other hand as Alex slashed at the vines around his feet.

I shoved Pearson towards Alex and Baracus, figuring that the two of them could defend Pearson if he needed to.

I was hit from behind so hard I flew off the path. I landed on the lawn and rolled to my feet.

I had been struck by a topiary. One of the shaped bushes—this one a rhino—had rammed into me.

It stamped its feet and lowered its head, ready to run me over again.

It's a distraction. Get off the grass.

I didn't trust the ground I stood on, so I threw my upper body forwards in a roll. I almost made it to the path when I crashed into another bush. This one a crab. It took damage by stopping me, but it leaped on me, snapping for my body, not piercing my armor.

The ground rippled around me and reached up, grabbing my shoulders and pinning me down. I began to sink, head first, into the dirt.

The lawn is trying to eat me.

The rhino roared and turned towards me, ready to trample me further into the dirt. Other topiary trudged in from around the lawn, circling the house. The house itself knew we were a threat and sent vines and bushes to defend itself against me.

What about the guards? I briefly thought as I fought against the topiary crab.

The back door to the house burst open. One of the Serpent men stood there, gun out. He drew down on me, and the weapon hummed. I realized that it was, once again, some sort of eldritch weapon ... the kind that punched through my armor during the attack the night before.

Hail Mary, full of Grace—

Inside the kitchen, the cigarette touched the matches in the matchbook. It set off a chain reaction in the sulfur and the potassium chlorate, setting alive a flame.

The natural gas, which was heavier than air, had come down to meet the flames.

The explosion started from the corner next to the door. The serpent was blasted out of the back door and into the air. It shot past Pearson and Baracus, slamming into the back wall. The flames blasted out, ripping out the door frame and the bricks around it. Flames blew out the windows of the kitchen.

The fire ripped through the rest of the first floor. The explosion from the buildup blasted out walls and consumed guards. Bushes too close to the house caught ablaze and screamed in pain. Flaming debris rained down all across the lawn, and the lawn writhed in pain like a living thing.

Most importantly, the lawn was so distracted that it let me go.

I sat up and threw the topiary crab away, into the back door. It went into the flames and didn't come out.

The rhino, however, was still mobile...and its back was on fire. Unlike the others, it was so focused on me as its target, it ignored the flames.

The flaming rhino charged me.

I was in no mood for anything fancy, so I reared back and struck the flaming rhino in the face. My armored fist punched into the topiary face. I grabbed internal branches and *pulled*. The head came off, and I threw it away. The bush wandered, blind.

I ran through the back gate as the house exploded again. This time, the explosion ripped through the entire building, blew out all of the walls, and collapsed the roof. The gas main had ruptured, and it spilled flaming debris all over the property.

We ran for the cliffs and didn't look back.

The four of us slid down the rope (yes, I slid down too. I wasn't going to levitate down when gravity did my job for me). When I stopped short of the deck, I armored down and dropped. "We're good to go. Baracus, get the boat started."

Baracus laughed. "I hear and obey, oh master!" He bounded off.

I rolled my eyes. "Don't you start with me," I called after him. I looked at my watch. "I need to hit the post office." I looked to Pearson. "What the Hell is a Tiamat?"

Alex looked at me for a moment, startled, then laughed once. "I thought you knew everything religious."

I rolled my eyes. "I'm Catholic, not professionally pagan."

Pearson shrugged and grabbed a hold of the deck above the wheel as the engine started. He leaned forward and called over the engine noise. "Ancient Babylonian 'goddess' of sea salt, mother of a lot of their pantheon, and embodiment of primordial chaos. Supposedly also gave birth to dragons who had poison in their veins instead of blood."

Alex groaned and smacked his head. He muttered. "Just great. It's a breeder. Just what they need to cover all the lands of Earth in darkness."

Pearson nodded. "It's probably the point of raising it."

Alex growled to himself and clenched his fist. "So, all this, everything we just did, tells us nothing."

From the bridge, Baracus looked over his shoulder and called back to us. "On the contrary! It tells us everything." He glanced at the water every phrase or two to keep track of where we were going. "Demons are pure being. They can only manifest a physical form by co-opting other matter. It's why possession is more common. Tiamat? She's associated with sea salt. It's probably back from the days when giants walked the Earth, she came forth from the water. As most of the matter on Earth is water, this group of demons will manifest by the ocean. On or overlooking a beach, perhaps."

Alex looked at him with surprise, as though it was strange he would be useful at all.

"Is that how you would do it?" he called forward.

Baracus stared out at the water for a long time and didn't answer. When he looked back at Alex, he narrowed his eyes and sneered with the air of a man whose professional pride had been hurt. "No. I would use a mountain as the matter, miles away from where we are now, so you could never find us." He looked front again, at the water. "But these people are amateurs and shallow."

Alex frowned. "If you hate these people so much, why do you work for them?"

Baracus scoffed without looking back at us. "I follow the money. And I owe service to others as part of deals with my Friends on the Other Side. But do you think I would have a use if so many were patient and knowledgeable about such things? People want arcane, forbidden knowledge, but they want to put in none of the effort. They wish to plug a quarter into a vending machine, punch a button, and have them spit out riches and power. I am the vending machine."

Alex snorted. "Kids today, am I right? No work ethic."

I took a deep breath and shook my head. "Doesn't matter. We have shoreline, but in case no one noticed, we've got miles of coastline to search. We're in Massachusetts. The entire Eastern border of the state is the Atlantic."

At that moment, my phone buzzed against my chest. I was tempted not to answer it, because I didn't want to answer too close to the edge of the boat—and the safest place was next to Baracus. I sighed. It was probably important. I trudged forward, keeping my face from the spray. I pulled out the phone.

It was Mariel.

"Hi, honey!" I exclaimed.

"We made it to the beach," she informed me calmly.

Is there screaming in the background? Must be a party. I smiled. "That's great! Minniva got away okay?"

"Yes, but ... there's a bonfire on the beach you might want to check out."

I blinked. She was calling about a *bonfire?* "What makes you think so?"

"First, I don't think that bonfires are legal here. I also don't think they're supposed to be fifty feet high and climbing."

WE MADE A STOP ON THE WAY TO THE BEACH. A QUICK STOP. IT had been tempting to swing by the beach directly, but we needed the supplies. Not to mention that if we arrived in the middle of the arrival of Tiamat from the ocean, there would have been no advantage to arriving by boat. Even Alex said, "No thanks. I've seen the original Japanese *Godzilla*. Boats fare even worse in that than they do in *Jaws*."

Our car was a few beaches away from where Mariel was parked. We got to the car and made a trip to Costco.

The day that started sunny had become overcast, gray and dark, ready to thunder and lightning. Heck, it became darker than during our expedition into Matchett's house. In a few more minutes, it would look pitch black.

As we drove for the beach, Alex asked, "How are we going to find where the problem is?"

I turned a corner and nearly ran into a woman in a bikini screaming as though a swarm of angry bees chased her. She didn't even stop long enough to ask for help; she just kept running away and screaming.

She wasn't the only one. A small mob ran right after her.

However, they weren't going after her in particular. Once they hit the main intersection, they flocked in three different directions. Wherever they wanted to be, it was far, far away from the beach.

Pearson looked at Alex. "I think we found the problem," he said dryly.

We cruised through the mob. It was slow going, but faster than walking. The mob scattered around us, barely acknowledging our existence. Our car was just another obstacle.

Alex leaned forward between me and Baracus (a man that tall was not sitting in the back of the car). He wanted a better view of the screaming mob. "Did the demon show up yet?"

"No," Pearson answered from the back seat. "The ritual has begun in earnest. It may be close to being finished. Maybe thirty minutes until the end."

I didn't ask him to elaborate on *the end*.

Baracus shrugged. "Yes. It happens. Physically manifesting a demon can drive anyone mad."

I frowned, thinking back to a conversation I once had with Auxiliary Bishop Xavier O'Brien. "XO referred to them as a Cthulhu for that reason. Just seeing it can drive you insane."

Pearson snorted from the back seat. "That's putting it mildly. But this is just the ritual."

Alex leaned back to face Pearson. "How can you tell?"

Baracus snorted from the front seat. "Because Tiamat is not already here."

Alex leaned over to see out the side window. A set of cliffs ran behind the beach at the other end from the entrance. "It could be behind the cliffs."

Pearson sighed. "The cliffs couldn't hide it. It would be too big."

Alex groaned. "Oh come on. That's just not fair. How are we supposed to beat something like that?"

I didn't answer him and neither did Pearson. I focused on the mob in front of us. I also focused on the package that was on its way.

Pearson had reached out to track the package sent from Rome. It was already three o'clock, and it was supposed to be arriving around now. But if we had a chance to stop the ceremony and prevent Tiamat from rising, the package could be labeled "return to sender."

If we didn't stop it, I had a backup plan.

We pulled into the parking lot, which was now practically empty. There were several possible reasons—like everyone had gone insane and fled. However, it was possible my family in the middle of the parking lot made everyone nervous. They all wore bathing suits. Lena wore something in pink. Jeremy had purple swim trunks (colored after his favorite Ninja Turtle). The good Doctor Holland wore a simple black bikini that was tasteful as far as bikinis went, though Alex looked like his eyes were going to pop out of his head. Mariel had a tasteful one-piece red bathing suit that made me want to take it off of her ... okay, that's not true, everything she wore made me want to take it off of her.

However, every last one of the women and children held an AR-15.

Mariel held hers one-handed. Grace, in a tiny bright-blue one-piece, was in her other arm. Lena had a hot pink Hello Kitty AR-15 that she clung to like it was a teddy bear. Jeremy had a GI Joe wrap on his. Mariel and Sinead went with basic black.

They were all backlit by the bonfire Mariel had mentioned on the phone. The bonfire was about a mile away, but massive enough to highlight my family. It was dramatic and would have been a Kodak moment for the kids if it weren't for the time issue.

We pulled up a car length away and got out. I had explained to Mariel over the phone that Baracus was on our side, for the time being. Everyone but Lena and Grace still looked like they considered test-firing a few rounds in Baracus' face.

Baracus grinned and bowed. "A pleasure to see you all again." He looked to Lena. "You're new. What's your name, little girl?"

Lena stared at him a moment, as though peering into his soul— which she could do, and I wouldn't have advised. She said something in a language that was not Polish – perhaps French? Baracus straightened sharply and looked away from Lena. He took one long sidestep behind me, as though using me for a shield. I should have told him it wouldn't have worked.

I looked around at the rest of the beach behind them. There was blood on sand and surf. Bodies were strewn on the beach. A collection of survivors huddled away from the water, at the edge of the sand. They looked scared and beaten.

"What happened here?" I asked.

Mariel stared at Baracus for another long moment before she looked to me and sighed. Her body sagged after holding in the stress for so long. "The fire went up hours ago, down the beach. No one cared. I don't even think anyone reported it. It was a curiosity. I don't even think I cared at first. Then it grew until it looked like, well, that. Then the chanting started. About half the beach went insane. They drove off most of the sane ones, except for what you see behind you. We shot a few of the crazies, and they had enough sense to leave us alone. Half the crazies went after the sane, and the other half headed *towards* the bonfire."

I frowned, then looked to the priest and the bokor. "Why only half?"

Baracus shrugged. "I presume half of them went to church." He shrugged. "It's why secularization was so heavy on Matchett's to-do list these last decades. If America were half as faithful as it were 70 years ago... even twenty years ago, when people when to church again after 9-11... this might be easily prevented just by the strength of local faith." He smiled a little, smirking at a memory of long ago. "Trust me, I had to work much harder back then. But I was also paid more."

I blinked, trying to imagine what his life—okay, unlife—was like back in the 1950s, but I turned back to my wife and kids. "Time to leave, honey."

Mariel looked at me a moment. She shared a glance with Sinead and said, "You owe me ten." She looked back at me. "Are you insane? The crazies are probably stalking the ways out of here. We have guns and can support you. We'll be behind you." She glanced over her shoulder at the bonfire and looked back. "Far behind you. If you fail, we're all going to die anyway. Might as well go together." She looked at Baracus. "Can't you make yourself useful? Make an army of zombies from the dead back there?"

The bokor shook his head. "I could. But it would take time we do not have. Nor do I know if it would be effective against the forces allied against us."

Mariel rolled her eyes. "We're *asking* you to make zombies, and you say no. Some villain!"

I looked past my family at the bonfire. While I could not count how many people there were around the flames, they swarmed the beach. There could have been a riot.

Good thing I have riot-quelling gear.

I walked towards the trunk and popped it open. Inside it was our Costco purchase, which included a twenty-dollar, fifty-pound bag of sea salt.

Mariel followed me to the trunk. "Are we having a cookout after? For ninety?"

"Because holy salt is a thing and it's twenty bucks in bulk."

I looked back to the bonfire, trying to make a plan that would let us complete the objective. Creating a plan that would allow us to live was impossible. According to Minniva Atwood's numbers, there were at least a hundred people down, probably closer to two hundred, and that was before the beach went insane.

But down by the bonfire end of the beach, about a mile away, was the cliff Alex looked at earlier. The cliff dropped down to a sandy beach. But on top of the cliff, and a bit back from the edge, was a small chapel.

"What's with the church?" I asked.

Baracus laughed. "It's to be destroyed first thing after Tiamat is raised from the ocean. What else?" he asked, as though that was self-evident common knowledge.

But the edge of the cliffs looked like a great perch for what I had in mind.

I looked to Mariel. I patted her on the arm and gave her a little squeeze. Then I kissed her on the cheek.

"Give me a moment," I said softy.

I waited until everyone turned their attention to the bonfire and the scene before us. I stayed back by the trunk. I bowed my head and prayed for God's blessing. I also prayed for some backup. It had worked once, without my meaning to, in the middle of London. It had been a long night, where Jihadis had tried to rip me apart and came to do violence to God's church and kill me.

Heavenly King, You have given us archangels to assist us during our pilgrimage on earth.

Saint Michael is our protector; I ask him to come to my aid, fight for all my loved ones, and protect us from danger.

Saint Gabriel is a messenger of the Good News; I ask him to help me clearly hear Your voice and to teach me the truth.

Saint Raphael is the healing angel; I ask him to take my need for healing and that of everyone I know, lift it up to Your throne of grace and deliver back to us the gift of recovery.

Help us, O Lord, to realize more fully the reality of the archangels and their desire to serve us.

Holy angels, pray for us. Amen.

I waited a moment, hoping that this would be an easy fix for what was to come.

After a long, long moment, longer than we had, nothing happened.

I straightened up and rolled my neck. That a host of angels had not clamored to our side didn't worry me. In fact, it reassured me. It meant that we had the tools we needed to stop Tiamat, two hundred demons, and hundreds of deranged maniacs.

I stepped around the car and clapped my hands together. "Okay, everyone, we're going to use that church. We're going to need both cars. Let's get to work. It's *Deus Vult* o'clock."

As a homicide detective, I rarely needed to dissemble. Given my faith, I am reluctant to lie. It's why I let Alex do the paperwork. Though given my abilities and the things I've encountered, I had become good at answering questions in ways that were technically accurate and, yet, didn't reveal anything. Had I been raised by early Jesuits, they would have been proud. However, the Opus Dei who home-schooled me would have been just as happy, I think.

However, I tended to be direct in all things. It made life much simpler. Being direct meant I didn't have to coordinate as much. It was high risk, but the situation was already so bad that I didn't see it being much riskier than any other option.

I walked up to the orgy of madness with my hands in my pockets. The madmen didn't notice me because they were mad. Many of the possessed didn't even look up from the bowing and scraping they did in the sand. They were all on their knees, bowing their heads to the sand as though they worshiped the bonfire. I hadn't seen anything like it outside of using prayer rugs—or documentaries about Imperial China, where they would bow to the Emperor like that.

As I got closer to the center of the insanity, an inner circle recited aloud from various books. All of the books present I had seen in the library of George Matchett.

Now we know what he needed with all of those books.

Standing before the bonfire, facing the acolytes, was Professor Noah Whateley. He had changed out of his smoking jacket into a robe of brilliant scarlet. His hood was back, so I saw him clearly in the light from the flames. Whateley read aloud from the Necronomicon.

The only phrase I caught was *Ia! Ia!Cthulhu Fhtagn! Ia! Ia!*

I was only ten yards away when I stopped. A gentle breeze blew behind me. I let it carry my call to Whateley. "So, Professor. Do I call you Curran? Or do I call you Legion?"

The Professor stopped reading aloud and glanced at me. He locked on my face for a long moment. He didn't break eye contact as he slowly closed the Necronomicon and lowered it to the sand.

And he smiled. The smile was the last thing I needed. I knew I was right. Ever since Gerald Downey referred to me, derisively, as "saint," I'd had a dark suspicion the demons involved knew me. When Minniva mentioned Rikers, I knew that my name had at least gone the rounds in the underworld. When Whateley knew me by sight, I was almost certain.

But that smile proved it to me. The smile wasn't Whateley's smile. It was Christopher Curran's smile. It was the smile I had seen the first time I had died a violent death. It was the smile I had never wanted to see again.

"Saint," he said.

I smiled at him. "No, I don't think you qualify."

Whateley tilted his head towards me, as if to ask if I was serious. "I mean you."

I shrugged and looked around at his cronies. They hadn't even looked at us. "I'm not dead yet."

"We *can* fix that. We have a few minutes. The process has already begun, you cannot stop it. Or us." Whateley looked around at the others. As one, the ones with the books stopped their chanting.

They delicately closed the books, gently set them aside in the sand, and rose. They were so mechanical and so coordinated about it, I knew they were one mind. One thought. One legion.

Whateley smiled at the backup, ready to attack me. He glanced at me. "How did you know it was us?"

I shrugged. "Other members of your legion also called me 'saint.' Also, I had a talk with Minniva. Nice girl. You should have left her out of it. If you had, we would have been left out of it. She told me you jerks were still pissed about Rikers."

Whateley rolled his eyes. "Corporate incompetence. She got the wrong email. Everyone at the black mass was specifically picked for the ceremony." He waved around the beach at the calm, placid possessed. "Some of the people you see here are my colleagues from the university. They also joined in."

I sighed and shook my head, as I would with any three-time loser. "Wasn't it bad enough to get your ass kicked last time?"

Whateley smiled at me. "No. This time, I have backup from a far more reliable source." He waved at the possessed. "No warlocks. No bokors. No stupid cults. This time, I phoned home directly."

I nodded slowly. Many of the possessed looked suddenly uncomfortable. Some started to sweat. Some coughed. A few even fought back a bored yawn.

I met Whateley's gaze. "I didn't know Matchett was that smart." I leaned in conspiratorially. "Or did he have help thinking of the idea?"

Whateley smiled, then stopped to fight back a yawn of his own. He covered his mouth with a fist, then shook his head like a wet dog to fight it off. He blinked a little, fighting irritation in his eyes. "I will grant you, that yes, the body of Chris Curran *may* have sent off an email to George Matchett. It *may* have made a suggestion about a grand finale before Matchett's end." Whateley shrugged and gestured at all of the books from the billionaire's collection. "Matchett had already been putting a plan in motion. We merely helped him refine it a little. He needed little help from us."

I found it interesting how his personal pronouns had shifted away to a more collective way of speaking. "Do you even have a name?"

Whateley shrugged. "What's in a name?"

I looked around at everyone from the possessed. Each and everyone one of them looked at me with the same level of loathing. It was almost the same expression on a hundred different faces. The only difference was how many sweated, how many coughed and how many yawned.

"I'm told demons are usually far more subtle than...this."

Whateley laughed and flung his hands up. "So I have a flair for style. So what?" He shrugged. "Besides, the cult who raised me wanted a bogeyman. And when I found you ... well, you were someone I could put on a *show* for. The cult wanted mass possession of Rikers. *Curran* needed to be in jail. *We* needed time to see who could be possessed in the general population. What was the harm in showing off?" He paused and yawned again. He fought it off and kept going. He wandered a little closer to me, grinning big. "There are so few exorcists kicking around. By the time most *people* would have figured it out, Hoynes would have locked the Catholic church out of the city, if not the state, so who could *do* anything about it? The Vatican's ninjas?"

I arched my brows. I had been directly told that there were no such things as ninjas at the Vatican. I would have made a note to ask Auxiliary Bishop O'Brien, but it wasn't that important in the short run.

Whateley took a deep breath but fought back another yawn. He sighed and nodded, rolling his eyes all at the same time. "Okay. *Maybe* involving you was a mistake. But how was *I* to know you'd have the charism to cast out demons ... *and* have a list of priests in your call tree?"

Then the vomiting started.

Whateley turned around. One of his possessed dropped to the sand and vomited. He was coughing up nails. Another one dropped next to Whateley and nails came out. The vomit was sporadic, and all over the gathering. Whateley looked frantically from person to person. He finally noted that his possessed were afflicted with sweating mucus, or coughing, or yawning, or vomiting up objects that had cursed them.

Whateley whirled on me, his face a familiar mask of hate and rage. "Wait. What have you done?"

I smiled beatifically in his face. "I'm a distraction."

IF YOU HAVE A GOOD MEMORY AND HAVE READ THE CHRONICLES of my supernatural battles, you would notice one constant theme. Generally, I do not land the final blow. With the exception of a certain shootout in King's Point, Long Island, the solution to the problem was never a bullet or a bomb. It had always been the hand of God. Sometimes it was holy water and exorcism. Once it was a fireball from Heaven. Or angels. Or an artifact from before time. Or an army of golems.

In this case, part of the solution was a bag of sea salt bought wholesale.

My plan was simple. Jeremy would take Grace and hole up in the church. It would be the fallback position of last resort and a gathering place if we had to exfiltrate from the area in a hurry.

Mariel took up position behind the church, at cliffside, with her AR-15 and a rosary wrapped around the hand that gripped the rifle stock. I had suggested that she shoot to the rhythms of the *Hail Marys*, or *Glory Bes* if rapid fire were required.

The most important part of the plan went to Doctor Sinead Holland. She knew the area best and took her car out to the local post office. Pearson had the address, and she knew the path. Her mission was to retrieve the package from Rome, then get it back to me.

Sinead was off and driving within a minute of our arrival at the beach.

But Sinead was merely the backup. If everything went wrong,

her mission was going to be our last chance, short of an orbital strike from Heaven.

But, before that, before anything else, the opening gambit of the plan belonged to both Father Pearson and Lena.

My ward stood on the cliff between our two snipers and focused her mind on one thing and one thing alone—generating a soft, gentle breeze. The breeze was barely noticeable amid the racing wind by the water, the waves crashing closer and closer to us on the beach, or all of the chanting. Had any of them noticed, they might have felt that the breeze went one way while the winds everywhere else blew another.

On this gentle, soft breeze floated a light mist of blessed holy salt.

Further down the beach, within sight of only madmen, was Father Pearson, praying the rite of exorcism at the entire crowd around the bonfire. All of them were focused on me, so none of them had even tried to put up resistance.

I armored up, the golem armor covering me from head to toe. I said one word, that my armor amplified loud enough so that it reached Lena on the cliffs above.

"Maelstrom."

Then the wind *really* picked up.

The gentle breeze was for two reasons. First, to introduce the holy salt so slowly that none of the possessed noticed an assault was going on. The second reason was to avoid kicking salt in my eyes.

The storm of holy salt that Lena unleashed with her mind was almost like a tornado, a maelstrom six feet high and wide enough to cover most of the beach. Yawning possessed had salt dumped in their mouths. Possessed who were still standing took salt right in their eyes, blinding them with a scream.

The bullets started flying then. Mariel opened fire from above. Unlike the battle in Rikers, there weren't thousands of other candidates ready to be possessed if someone had died. Most of the possessed down here had all wanted this. Whateley said as much.

They had wanted the power. They had wanted the rewards of the damned.

They had wanted Hell.

We were going to give it to them.

At the edge of the circle of madness were Bokor Baracus and Alex Packard. Alex opened fire into the crowd, mowing them down with as many bullets as he could fire. He only went for headshots. The mad were fresh bodies for the demons. The demons were ... demons. Either way, they were fodder for Alex's gun. He also stood between Pearson and the ring of death. Pearson was the big gun.

Baracus and Alex had one job. They were to target anyone who wasn't debilitated by the onslaught of holy salt and prayers by Pearson. Alex protected Pearson from any who could make their way out of the salt storm.

Baracus, with a face mask and goggles, was to go into the salt storm.

Whateley whirled on me and roared, "You'll die for this!"

I drove my armored fist into his face so hard I spun him around. "Dying for salvation? Gladly." I grabbed him by the shoulder and headbutted him with my helmet to his face. "No capitulation."

Whateley came in with a right hook for my face. I blocked it with my left. I decked him in the face with my left hook as I blocked an uppercut with my right. I shot both hands forward and grabbed his neck and his shoulder, then drove my knee into his guts.

Whateley bent over, and charged me, plowing me into the dirt. He straddled my armored chest and pounded into my face. The clay cracked and shifted, reforming to keep up with the endless pounding. The blows drove my head in to the sand without any remorse or letting up.

MEANWHILE, BOKOR BARACUS CHARGED INTO THE MAELSTROM of salt and sand. He wore a medical mask to cover his mouth and nose. He wore goggles to keep the salt out of his eyes. And he led with a machete. Heads flew left and right. He was a blur of speed and strength. When we had fought in the past, he had let his arrogance overcome his good judgment. This time, he wasn't holding back. He was an endless whirl of death. He took a leg so hard and fast, he swept a demon off his feet, into the air, and took the head off before the body hit the ground.

Bokor Baracus swept through the mad and the possessed like a plague of rats through a cheese factory. Athame in one hand, inverted against his forearm, and the machete in the other, he went to work at what he did best.

The first possessed blocked his overhead blow with a forearm. Baracus slashed him across the belly with the athame, cutting open the artery just off the aorta, and then whirled to his left, the possessed already dead to him. He pivoted on his right foot, to launch a round-house kick to the man on his right, and the machete decapitated another on his left as he swirled around.

As Baracus's left foot touched the ground, his athame arced down and across the throat of the person in front of him. The machete followed with another decapitation strike on his right. As the pommel came down, it knocked aside the body in front of him, clearing the way for a snap-kick to the throat in front. The machete, hardly even decelerated from its swing, changed direction and arced up, under the chin of the man on his left and coming down on the skull to his right. Another pivot allowed Baracus to cut another throat in front of him, break the neck to his left with a roundhouse, and he lunged forward with the blade in a great arc, sweeping aside everyone in front of him and killing someone else on his right.

It was a thing of terrifying elegance. Baracus was a whirling dervish, no movement wasted, and no hesitation. Each move constantly flowed into the other like a dance of death. It was much like watching the ballet, and with every swing of an arm, someone else died. He was efficient and unstoppable. Everyone with a blunt instrument was mowed down like wheat, unable to stand up to the athame. Anyone who wielded a sharp object had nothing to stop the machete. No one had a gun.

"A PITY." WHATELEY THREW ANOTHER RIGHT FOR MY HEAD, snapping it to one side. "There won't even be a world left after Tiamat is done with you. No papal commendation for you. Just annihilation."

"Fine," I spat. He threw a left, I slipped it, jerking my upper body to the right. Whateley punched the sand so hard, he buried his arm up to his elbow. I hooked the arm with my left and bucked my hips so hard I flipped him. I rolled to my feet. "Heaven is my target destination anyway."

I smiled through my heavy breathing. I was winded but still ready to battle Whateley to the death. The mad and the possessed had fallen around us for several yards. Mariel had been busy. She fired with such rhythm, I could even hear the praying.

Hail Mary. Double-tap.

Full of Grace. Bang.

The Lord is with thee. Bang. Bang. Bang.

Whateley leaped for me. I leaped for him. We collided in mid-air in front of the bonfire. As the clouds gathered and darkened, the bonfire was the only true source of light.

As we grappled, we threw knees, elbows, head butts. He could never punch through my armor. I could never damage him enough to disable even an arm. But it didn't matter. As long as I fought the lead demon, at the focal point of the ceremony, every demon had eyes on me—assuming that they could see through the maelstrom Lena had created.

Then, like a killer from a slasher movie, Bokor Baracus leaped out of the cloud, machete and athame held high. He screamed something in French, heading straight for Whateley.

Unfortunately, from the water charged something else. Something eight feet tall and four feet wide, with horns even wider still. It seemed like a Minotaur, charging in like the bull he resembled. He body checked Baracus and flung him into the air. He didn't stop moving, and his shoulder glanced me and Whateley. The glancing blow was so powerful it bowled over both of us.

The Minotaur kept charging and slammed Bokor Baracus into the side of the cliffs.

It was not a Minotaur, but Kusarikku. He was a spawn of Tiamat who had preceded "her." Kusarikku had the arms, torso, and head of a human; but the ears, horns and hindquarters were solid bull. As Tiamat represented sea salt in its mythology, Kusarikku represented mountains. Like the cliffs that it pummeled Baracus into.

I swept up the Necronomicon with both hands and whirled on Whateley, smashing him in the face with it.

Then with a whirl, I hurled the book into the bonfire.

Whateley's eyes went wide, and he hurled himself after the book.

I turned away from both the professor and the book and charged after Kusarikku and Baracus. My helmet's display highlighted the monster from the depths as I bounded for it. Kusarikku showed up with his name and as a "summoned demon," and that was it. No suggestions on how to fight it. No thoughts on what to do with it once I got my hands on it.

I reared back with my fist and prayed, picking Psalm 5.

Give ear to my words, O LORD; understand my sighing.

Kusarikku was one more bound away, and I made it.

Attend to the sound of my cry, my king and my God!

I drove my fist into the back of Kusarikku's head. Its human face drove into the cliff wall, leaving an additional hole right next to Baracus'.

For to you I will pray, LORD; in the morning you will hear my voice; in the morning I will plead before you and wait.

Kusarikku whirled on me and backhanded me away. I went flying back twenty feet. And Kusarikku followed hot on my trail. A fist the size of my head crashed into my chest armor, caving it in. The blow sent me back along the sand. My armor couldn't heal the wound before the next swing came in. I sheltered the wound with my left arm. Kusarikku drove its fist into my bicep.

My arm broke with a *crack* so loud, it could be heard over the breaking of my armor.

You are not a god who delights in evil.

I groaned in pain and wheeled around, twisting my entire body into the punch. I drove my right fist into Kusarikku's face and kept my wounded side away from the demon.

Kusarikku smiled.

No wicked person finds refuge with you.

I ducked under the next swing, and leaped up, driving my knee into Kusarikku's face. The blow sent it back a step. I came down with both armored feet, smashing into its foot.

The arrogant cannot stand before your eyes.

Kusarikku grunted and bent over, running its nose into my right elbow.

You hate all who do evil. I backhanded it.

You destroy those who speak falsely. I drove the sole of my boot into its knee. I kicked off of the leg, jumping back instead of breaking the knee.

A bloody and fraudulent man the LORD abhors. Kusarikku came in and casually swatted me in the chest plate. The armor had healed itself enough that the blow sent me sprawling instead of killing me.

Kusarikku rose over me. And it laughed.

But I, through the abundance of your mercy, will enter into your house.

Baracus leaped on its back and drove his athame into its shoulder. The blade punctured down to the hilt. Kusarikku bled seawater and roared in pain.

I will bow down toward your holy sanctuary out of fear of you.

Kusarikku whirled around, trying to get Baracus off of it. The bokor wouldn't budge. He locked his arm around Kusarikku's neck like a vice. He pulled out the athame and stabbed Kusarikku again and again, laughing at the demon's pain.

LORD, guide me in your justice because of my foes; make straight your way before me.

My armor *clicked* as the last plate of clay slid into place. Then it worked on fixing my arm. I grit my teeth against the pain and pushed myself up. I wasn't going to let Baracus fight Kusarikku alone.

The wind picked up. A burst of holy salt the size of a cannon ball smashed Kusarikku right in the face. Lena had seen the way the battle had been going and decided to focus on us a little. The salt burned the demon with a snap and a sizzle that sounded like meat hitting a fry pan. It cried out in agony.

For there is no sincerity in their mouth; their heart is corrupt.

I darted in swinging. I delivered three quick body blows with my fists, and followed it up with a low roundhouse kick to Kusarikku's leg that would have felled a tree.

It all did nothing.

Their throat is an open grave; on their tongue are subtle lies.

I jumped up and drove my right fist into Kusarikku's face, where the salt still clung. Its head snapped back, and more water came from its lip. That hurt it.

Declare them guilty, God; make them fall by their own devices.

A path opened up in the salt maelstrom. I feared for a moment that the mad or the possessed had found a way to create an opening.

Instead, it was Alex. Pearson was right behind him. Pearson read from his prayer book. Alex ran in, hand in his pocket.

"Hey asshole, pick a card!" Alex screamed, and his hurled a metal saint card into Kusarikku's side.

The holy card bit into Kusarikku's flesh like it had cut into the fruit yesterday morning when Lena had thrown it with her mind. The blessing burned through the demon's hide like a hot knife through water.

Drive them out for their many sins; for they have rebelled against you.

I drove my fist into Kusarikku's side where the card bit in. It shrieked and hurled Baracus off at long last. It whirled around to face Alex, and I jumped onto its back the way Baracus had. I grabbed Kusarikku's horns and bent him back, opening him up to Alex throwing four more cards in quick succession.

Then all who trust in you will be glad and forever shout for joy.

As I struggled against Kusarikku, I endeavored to rip its head off with the horns. "For the grace ... for the might of our Lord ... in the name of His Glory ... time for you to go back to Hell."

Without warning, Whateley smashed into me, driving me off of Kusarikku. We went sprawling across the sand and crashed into the cliffside. Baracus took my place to tangle against Kusarikku as Whateley pounced on me.

You will protect them and those will rejoice in you who love your name.

Whateley raised an undamaged Necronomicon over his head and brought it down onto my chest. The clay armor smashed like glass against the enchantments and dark magic of the book. He drove the book into my chin and ripped the helmet right off of my face.

Whateley loomed over me and threw the book aside. My face and chest were wide open. "I don't think so. I'm the only god here today. And my name is death." He raised his arms together, both hands folded together into one fist. "And what do you say to the god of death?"

His hands came down as my hands shot up. The gloves and arms of the armor acted together to clamp onto Whateley's hands. The armor locked and held fast. They were mechanical grips against an organic force.

I smiled in his face, just to piss him off. "Not yet."

I twisted my body, and threw Whateley away like the garbage he was.

For you, LORD, bless the just one; you surround him with favor like a shield.

I clamored to my feet. Kusarikku threw Baracus off to one side, leaving Alex as the only thing between him and Pearson.

I charged Kusarikku, moving as fast as I could on sand.

But Kusarikku charged Alex and Pearson, his head bowed, the horns aimed right for my partners.

Kusarikku was faster.

The horns speared through both Pearson and Alex. The horn pierced Alex in the right ribcage, leaving a hole the size of a softball in his chest. The cards fell from his hands as he was taken off his feet, and he screamed. Pearson was run through the stomach.

Kusarikku pinned them both up against the cliff-side. Blood came out of Alex's mouth in great globs. Pearson only had a little leaking from his lip.

Kusarikku ripped his head out of the wall and out of both of my partners. They dropped to the ground, bleeding out right in front of me.

I ran towards them. I had once healed Mariel when her throat had been slit. *Maybe if I—*

Motion in my right eye caught my attention. One of the dead bodies had started to move. I looked to Baracus, and he was still getting to his own feet.

Bokor said that raising zombies might not work against demons. Which means...

I glanced at the dead rising. The wounds in their heads were healing. They weren't being raised as zombies. They were coming back *as* the possessed they were.

Dying had only slowed them down.

The bluetooth earbud in my ear rang. It had been held in place by the armored helmet. It automatically picked up, even as I staggered towards Pearson and Alex.

"Sinead?" I answered as I stumbled in the sand. "Tell me you have the package!"

I was answered by a roar of wind and rain that sounded like solid static. "—ommy! I—" Sinead cut out for a moment. "—the package. The rain—" The flickering signal went dead for a full four seconds, which felt like four minutes.

The signal came back in. "*I can't get to you!*" came through crystal clear.

I blinked. The package was lost.

I crawled to Alex and Pearson and laid hands on them, and quickly prayed, ripping through an *Our Father* and a *Hail Mary*.

It wasn't working. Either I was too distracted, or the answer was a simple, "No."

Either way, my partners were dying.

Whateley had gotten to his feet and laughed at me. "Poor little saint. Can't save anyone. Can you? And you thought that you were going to save the world?"

Ten-foot waves crashed down on the shoreline. The sea became choppier. The winds picked up, blowing away all of the holy salt and sand from Lena's maelstrom. Lighting crackled all around me.

And out in the water, several lines broke through the surface of the water. They emerged as fins. But they weren't from sharks. They were serrated and elongated.

The fins broke through the water, and the smooth arc of heads started to come up. It was like seven kaiju were ready to break the surface any minute.

Each dragon head that broke through the surface was bigger than a house. Each head was a different color. From right to left, they were red, orange, yellow, green, blue, indigo and violet. Before it even rose out of the water, I knew that all of the necks snaked down to one trunk of a body.

Tiamat was rising.

THERE WAS NO WAY THAT I COULD HAVE FOUGHT THE POSSESSED rising around me, as well as Kusarikku, and Tiamat, *and* save my partners.

I had to stop Tiamat. Even if it killed me, and my family, and my friends. It had to go back to Hell.

Only without Sinead and the package she carried from Rome, there was nothing I could think of that could stop the Cthulhu demon.

Behind me, Whateley laughe at me. At us. At the world.

At God.

I'd had enough.

My golem arms were still intact, as were the legs. I pushed off my feet, flinging myself backwards, and driving my fist into Whateley's face so hard, it lifted him off of his feet. I reached down and grabbed his ankles in midair and twisted. I spun Whateley in the air by his ankles and made it through two rotations before I hurled Whateley and threw him into Kusarikku. The possessed professor and the demon hurtled down the beach, next to the massive bonfire.

"You think you've won?" I roared at them. I charged Kusarikku and drop-kicked it in the face. The Minotaur staggered back. I charged to my feet, then drop-kicked its knees. One leg went out from under it, dropping it to perfect uppercut height. I drove my fist into its chin, knocking the head back.

I whirled on Whateley and backhanded him with the gauntlet. One of his feet went flying. "As long as one of us still alive, you're doomed." I grabbed him by the lapels and headbutted him in the nose, crushing it. "All one of us needs is the Lord. What are *all* of you against Him?"

Whateley smashed his arms through my grip and shoved me away so hard I flew through the air. I landed in the sand and rolled. He straightened, smiled, and brushed some sand off of him. "Oh, we know. That's why we kill all of you first."

In the ocean, Tiamat flexed her wings.

The ocean parted in two tsunamis, one to either side. The one that went north crashed into the taller cliffs and broke off the cliff face.

The southbound tsunami swept through the parking lot, sweeping away half of the cars and crashing into the land. It came down on everything like a steamroller, flattening everything. There were three skyscrapers in its path, and they all toppled over like towers of Jenga blocks. There had been homes where the tsunami made landfall further down the beach. There was no sign of them when the wave passed. Even the foundations had been swept away.

I had only seen a glimpse of Tiamat before the waters rushed back in. Even the heads were massive.

Tiamat stomped down one step forward. The resulting tusnami was smaller this time, and headed away from shore, out to see. It took out three cargo ships, a dozen fishing boats. Even under the water, it shoved a submarine twenty miles off course. This didn't even include the countless sea life stunned or killed by the shockwave.

The clouds gathered so far and wide, it went to the horizon. There was no sun. The horizon itself was capped with clouds. They blocked the sun and turned the afternoon into night.

The gathering storm unleashed a barrage of lightning that

sounded like a bad day at Verdun – all of them, all at once. It destroyed the better part of Eastern Massachusetts. Each individual lightning bolt cratered a city block. And there were thousands of lightning bolts.

And Tiamat had just arrived.

God. I suspect I'm screwed. But I'd like to take this thing with us if you wouldn't mind.

My armored arms were still intact, so the first thing I did was charge Kusarikku. Without thinking, I leaped for him and kept going up. I grabbed his horns and levitated with the demon. It squealed in surprised as I took it off of its feet. I levitated over the bonfire and dropped Kusarikku into it.

Then, I kept levitating straight up.

Professor Whateley laughed at me as I flew away. He called after me, "Look down, saint! You get to watch me kill your friends!"

He looked down and stepped for Pearson and Alex, only to stop. Bokor Baracus stood between Whateley and my partners.

The bokor held his machete and his athame before him. His eyes narrowed, and he smiled, ready for a new fight. "No, demon. You will not."

Whateley scoffed at Baracus and waved him aside. "Get out of the way, bokor. You work for us. Hell owns you. *We* own you."

Baracus grinned at him. "Except that I have made a deal with Nolan. And these two behind me. And if I have nothing left, it is that I *keep my bargains.*"

Whateley blinked and took a step back. "You can't hope to win, Baracus."

The wide grin became evil. "I raised you and your legion once, demon. You bet I cannot send you *back?*"

I levitated up the cliff face, past everyone. I didn't wave back at Lena when she called out to me. I didn't even glance at my wife or at Sinead. I didn't have the time. I didn't have the seconds.

I levitated over to the church roof and landed on it. The stone crucifix on the roof faced Tiamat. The winds increased so heavily that my overcoat blew out, whipping around me in the maelstrom. The lightning cracked *past* me, even though I was the tallest point in the area. I grabbed the stone crucifix next to me, and braced myself against the rushing wind.

Tiamat kept coming, unabated. Nothing slowed her down. Lightning flashed past her, illuminating all seven heads. Lightning even struck two of the heads. She didn't even blink with the strike. The seas themselves became uneven and choppy as Tiamat passed, trying to rebel against this unnatural thing.

Tiamat's head towered over me, and she wasn't even out of the water yet. Her hips were still submerged beneath the waves. She was at least a mile tall and could destroy cities by walking past. She was taller than the tallest skyscraper. She was wider than the widest mountain.

She was death incarnate.

Dear God. If it is Your Will that this creature not destroy the world, then please, let us stop it now, before it gets to the rest of the world. Let not this terror from damnation be a scourge upon this Earth for one second more than it has to be. If I must die in order to do this— if we must all die in order to do this—then each of us is willing to do it... Okay, maybe not Baracus but certainly the rest of us.

Tiamat reared back and roared in defiance at God and Heaven. The red head shot balls of fire from her mouth to the sky. The orange unleashed a stream of fire. The mouth on the yellow dragon unleashed a torrent of lightning that lit up the clouds with electricity, which she distributed and unleashed back upon the Earth like a bombing run. The green mouth unleashed a stream of red-hot, boiling acid. The blue, indigo, and violet dragon heads unleashed streams that mirrored the heads on the other side.

For the grace, for the might of our Lord, in the name of His Glory. For the faith. For everything.

No Capitulation.

"Tiamat!" I bellowed. "As a sworn officer of the city of New York, I hereby place you under arrest. For murder. For sacrilege. For blasphemy." I looked down the beach as the wreckage from the tsunami became clearer. "For massive property damage. You have the right to remain silent, so shut your mouths."

When the monster stepped forward again, not slowing, I grabbed my handgun and drew down on it. I aimed for the middle head and emptied my gun in its direction.

"Hey, asshole! I'm talking to you!"

Tiamat dismissed me with a wave of her hand.

This meant that a wave of water kicked up from the ocean and slammed into me, even up on the cliff. I caught only the tail end of it, and that was enough to nearly knock me off of the church roof. I wrapped both arms around the crucifix next to me and held on for dear life. Mariel and Lena covered up and let the wave sweep them down back towards the church.

Hey, God. I meant what I said. But if you want this thing to win, let me know now so I can avoid the aggravation.

Then, over the sound of the wind and the rain and the lightning, over the sound of the footsteps and roaring of Tiamat, there was only one sound that gave me hope.

A car.

I turned. Pulling up to the church was what was left of Sinead Holland's car. There were no wheels left. The windows were broken. Water leaked from the trunk, from the engine block, and dripped out of the doors. Sinead opened the door and at least a bucket full of water spilled out.

Three men pushed the car forward. Despite the rain, they looked dry. One was in an army uniform, one was in scrubs, and the other looked like he was a mailman.

I blinked. *Well, I did say a prayer to angels. But sooner would have been better.*

Sinead got out of the car, package in hand, and reared back with it like a football. She hurled it for me.

Sinead threw like a girl. The package bounced off the side of the church.

However, the package came flying at me without any warning. Lena had grabbed it with her mind and hurled it at me. I caught it in the stomach with both hands, like a football.

I ripped off the packaging and smiled.

The package that I had ordered from Vatican City was a diamond—brilliant, translucent, and clear. There were natural, almost fluid striations on either side, within the stone itself. They were clearly below the gleaming, multifaceted surface. One set of striations was blood red. The other set was a startling silver. They were runes, written in the language of the angels. The silver runes were instructions on how to use the diamond for the greater glory of God. The blood red runes were a warning that disaster would befall anyone who used the stone improperly.

It was an artifact from before time. It had been handed to the first dynasty of Egypt by a creature that would be confused for a god. In time, it had destroyed the first capital city of the dynasty.

It was called the Soul Stone.

I raised the football-sized diamond before me and pointed one tip towards Tiamat. I looked into the eyes of the green, middle head and fought back the wave of madness that threatened to overwhelm me. I could go mad later.

I spoke without thinking. I spoke without needing to. The words that poured forth from me might as well have come from somewhere else.

"In the name of the Father, Jesus Christ"— I bowed my head at The Name. "His Son, and the Holy Ghost, I abjure you Tiamat! And cast you back to the pit from whence you came."

Despite being a speck compared to the mighty beast from Hell, the red dragon head turned its attention to me. Tiamat was not amused. The red spat a fireball at me and ignored me, like I was already dead.

The white hot ball of flame flashed across the distance between Tiamat and the church like lightning. It smashed into me, and the crucifix next to me. I disappeared into a cloud of fire and smoke.

When the smoke cleared, I was still there.

Tiamat stopped moving forward. The red and orange heads turned towards me. They were livid. But they were paying attention.

"In the name of John Paul the Great," I bellowed, "who defeated one of your thrones of Hell on Earth while he lived, I command you back to the abyss."

The left most head, the violet one, growled at me. With a voice that I would have imagined a tiger would have, roared back. "Who are you, little man, that you threaten me? Where were you when our Master, Lucifer, fell? Your world had barely formed. We were made to serve before any came to *be* served. We will eat your soul."

Just to emphasize the point, the orange head (second from Tiamat's right) let loose a stream of flame. It struck me dead on. It engulfed the church. It set the church grounds ablaze. The first ignited trees a dozen feet away. Even Sinead and Mariel had to put out the hems of their clothing, the heat was that intense.

The orange head cut the stream of fire and scoffed.

The fire cleared. The church was untouched, and so was I.

"I serve *the Lord*," I answered the fire. "He is my Sword and my shield! My guardian angel protects me. My patron, the defender of all police, is Michael the archangel himself, who cast Satan into Hell. Who the *Hell* are *you* against a single *one* of them? You wish to fight God? Who are you against the Lord?"

The Soul stone glowed. On the beach below, both the possessed and the mad shrank back from the light. Even Professor Whateley pushed away from Bokor Baracus in terror, falling away from the light of the Stone. They fell back even from Tiamat. They were scared of the Soul Stone and didn't want to be crushed by Tiamat.

All seven of Tiamat's heads gave me their full attention. They all spoke with one voice. They were loud enough to make my ears ring and my skull throb. "AND NOW YOU BURN FOR YOUR INSOLENCE!"

All seven heads let loose.

The red skull fired a stream of lightning. The orange mouth spit fireball after fireball. The mouth on the yellow dragon unleashed a torrent of violet flame. The green mouth unleashed a stream of red-hot, boiling acid. The blue, indigo, and violet dragon heads unleashed streams that mirrored the heads on the other side.

This time they aimed for me, the church, Lena, Sinead, and Mariel on the edge of the cliffs.

All seven attacks dispersed against the light from the Soul Stone. The light reached out and spread to the girls on the cliff.

"Come and get me!" I challenged them. "For I serve the Lord! And He will not let you pass. He commands you back to the depths of Hell. God wills it!"

Tiamat laughed and shook all seven heads, scoffing at me.

I ground my teeth and held the stone aloft. "O Glorious Prince of the heavenly host, St. Michael the Archangel, defend us in the battle against the principalities and powers, against the rulers of this world of darkness, against the evil spirits. Come to the aid of man, whom Almighty God created immortal, made in His own image and likeness, and redeemed at a great price from the tyranny of Satan."

Tiamat kept coming. The hips rose out of the water as she stepped forward. The heads towered over us even higher. "We curse you and all your line to eternal perdition."

The violet head darted forward like an adder to strike at me. Her teeth smashed against the light like a bulletproof bubble.

I continued my prayer to Michael the archangel, patron of the military and all police. "Fight this day the battle of the Lord, together with the holy angels, as already thou hast fought Lucifer and his apostate host, who were powerless to resist thee. That cruel, ancient serpent who seduces the whole world, was cast into the abyss with his horde."

Tiamat reached forth and punched at the light. It collided with the air as though stopped as though by a wall. "You will be hunted all the days of your life. You will never be rid of us."

So what else is new? I thought.

The light pulsed forward once more. And this time, the light itself came out *through* the rock of the cliff.

I leveled the stone at Tiamat like a gun. "Behold, this primeval enemy and slayer of men has taken courage. It wanders about, invading the earth to blot out the name of God and of His Christ, to seize upon, slay and cast into eternal perdition souls destined for the crown of eternal glory. This wicked dragon pours out, as a most impure flood, the venom of his malice on men of depraved mind and corrupt heart, the spirit of lying, of impiety, of blasphemy, and the pestilent breath of impurity, and of every vice and iniquity."

Lightning struck between the fingernails of Tiamat, as though the tips of its claws were Tesla coils. Balls of lighting formed and flew out, and all seven heads struck again this time. The attack stopped short of the rocks once more, the light stopping it hard. It spread out along the edge of the light like water on a windshield. It spread out and dispersed.

The next words out of my mouth reminded me of Bishop Ashley, and the evil of George Matchett, and the horrors proposed by the genuine Professor Whateley before his possession. "These most crafty enemies have filled and inebriated with gall and bitterness the Church, the spouse of the immaculate Lamb, and have laid impious hands on her most sacred possessions. In the See of Holy Peter where the Chair of Truth has been set up as the light of the world, they have raised the throne of their abominable impiety, in the hope that when the Pastor has been struck, the sheep may be scattered."

The flames and the lightning continued. Tiamat tried to press through the barrier. But now, the attacks no longer scattered as though striking a wall; they merely disappeared into the light. The light pushed forward, through the entire cliffside, even though it should have been casting a giant shadow.

Professor Whateley screamed, falling to the ground as though tortured. He fell over, not vomiting sea form and curses, but blood. He convulsed and thrashed on the ground as the demon was driven out of him, taking Whateley's life with it. Kusarikku climbed out of the bonfire, going right into the light, scattering into embers, even though the flames from moments before hadn't even scorched it.

All seven heads of Tiamat roared with the wrath of Achilles and the burning hatred of Satan himself. Tiamat reached down, under the surface of the ocean. It reached all the way down to the ocean floor and grabbed what it wanted.

It came up with a boulder bigger than the church itself. Tiamat raised the rock high above its heads and hurled it at us.

The rock clashed with the wall of light and disappeared into the brightness. A moment later, the rock came back out and shot forth at Tiamat, smacking into the green head in the middle. Tiamat staggered back, unsteady on its feet.

"Arise O invincible Prince!" I called, "against the attacks of these lost spirits to the people of God, and give them the victory. We venerate thee as our protector and patron. Holy Church glories you as her defense against the malicious power of hell; to thee has God entrusted the souls of men. And may vanquish the dragon, the ancient serpent, and make him captive again in the abyss, that he may no longer seduce the nations."

Tiamat held her hands in front of her, backing away. Before that particular moment, I wouldn't have imagined that a mile-tall lizard could look nervous. But this one managed it.

But Tiamat discovered, too late, that the light had surrounded her. The light closed in on all sides, like a cage. There was nowhere to run or retreat. She lashed out at the confinement. All the heads thrashed and expelled flame and lightning.

The light from the stone spread up as well as out and struck the clouds above. The clouds dispelled wherever the light touched.

The sunlight came down and highlighted the church and the cliff. "O God, the Father of our Lord Jesus Christ," I bowed my head once more, "we call upon Thy holy Name."

The Soul Stone unleashed a beam of light that burned away the rightmost head of Tiamat. The red dragon head burst into flame and disintegrated, all the way down the neck, into the trunk.

"We implore Thy clemency—" I continued.

The Stone let loose once more. It struck the orange neck, punching a hole through the middle. It blanched and reared back, shrieking as it disappeared in a tower of embers.

"That by the intercession of Mary, ever Virgin Immaculate and our Mother—"

The yellow head tried to dodge this time, but the beam of light seared through the neck at the base.

"And of the glorious St. Michael the Archangel—"

The Soul Stone focused on the other side of Tiamat this time, slashing through the violet head on the end. "Thou wouldst deign to help us against Satan—"

The indigo head roared, and the beam of light went straight down its throat. The light punched through the back of the head. It fell backwards, into the light cage, and burned away as it touched it.

"And all the other unclean spirits who wander the world to injure the human race and the ruin of souls."

The blue head tried to hide behind the red one. But again, it couldn't move its neck at the base. It sliced off like a squid losing an arm.

"Amen!"

Tiamat held out both of its hands to hold back the next strike. The Soul Stone blasted forth a final bright bream of light. Tiamat leaned into the beam, fighting against it with all of its being.

Tiamat's hands began to glow as the Soul Stone struck it, burning into it.

"The Most High God commands you ... God the Father commands you... God the Son commands you. God the Holy Ghost commands you... The sacred Sign of the Cross commands you ... The glorious Mother of God, the Virgin Mary, commands you... The faith of the holy Apostles Peter and Paul, and of the other Apostles commands you. The blood of the Martyrs and the pious intercession of all the Saints command you. Saint John Paul the Great commands! In the name of God! God wills it. For the grace, for the might of the

Lord, in the name of His Glory, go back to Hell and take your friends with you!"

Tiamat roared in defiance as the light of the stone punch through the palms of both hands. It struck the body of Tiamat full on. It punched through the monster and out the other side.

Tiamat screamed as the Stone sent her straight back to Hell.

THE WIND DISSIPATED. THE SEAS CALMED. THE SKY CLEARED. The lightning stopped.

The only sound remaining was my breathing.

The Soul Stone's runes glowed and hummed and slowly pulsed until the glow faded away.

The stone was still clear but like cloudy white quartz that did not interfere with the arcane runes or deep silver streaks, but it did look dull and spent. I put the Stone back in my pocket and slowly sat down on the roof. I let out my breath. I didn't even know I had been holding it.

I should have felt something. I should have felt the loss of Packard and Pearson. I should have felt elation at destroying a monster that would have destroyed the world. All I felt was the buzz of adrenaline. I felt drained. My next step was to take a nap.

Maybe taking a nap on the roof isn't out of line.

"Yo! Tommy?" came a bellow from the beach. "You might want to get down here!"

I blinked. That wasn't the voice of Baracus.

...Alex?

I dropped down from the roof. I landed like a feather. I ran for the cliff and jumped. I levitated down.

The beach was in turmoil.

The mad ones had been cured of their insanity. They were confused, wandering the beach, wondering what had happened. The possessed who had been killed were dead again without the demons within to keep them alive.

Both Alex and Father Pearson were alive. They were on their feet. Their wounds were healed, without even a hint of scar tissue.

However, Bokor Baracus was on his back in the sand. His skin had turned a mottled gray.

I walked over to his side. "Baracus?"

He looked at me through narrowed eyes. "It seems that your tool was so virtuous, it burned out all of the magic in my body." He tried to smile but didn't have the energy. He reached for his chest. He patted it twice, looking for something. He pulled the necklace out from his shirt. Whatever had been there was broken, only a jagged edge remained. "My phylactery." He breathed deeply, trying to keep speaking. "Shattered." He tried a shrug and failed.

Pearson stepped forward and knelt next to him. "Do you want last rites?"

Baracus raised a brow. "Do you think it will do any good?"

Pearson shrugged. "Usually. Best to err on the side of 'what's the harm?' I say." He made a sign of the cross over Baracus. "Into your hands, O Lord, we humbly entrust Bokor Baracus. In this life, you embraced him with your tender love ..." Pearson hesitated, wondering just how true the statement was. "Deliver him now from every evil and bid him eternal rest. The old order has passed away: welcome him into paradise, where there will be no sorrow, no weeping or pain, but fullness of peace and joy with your Son and the Holy Spirit forever and ever."

Baracus smiled. "Amen."

I looked him right in the eye and said, "Baracus, be good."

Baracus gave a faint smile: "Perhaps."

Then my greatest adversary, Baracus, the Voodoo bokor, died for the last time ... though for the first time, perhaps uncertain about his destination.

EVERYONE ON THE BEACH HAD EITHER RUN AWAY WHEN THE madness broke out, or were totally insane during the entire ordeal. Despite the effects of a manifest demon (inherent in labeling it "a Cthulhu"), the Soul Stone excelled at cleanup.

Bokor Baracus' body disintegrated. He went from "alive" to "full decomposition" in a matter of minutes. We used a cooler left on the beach to collect his remains before a gentle breeze could blow them away.

Once the cooler was locked tight, I hugged both Alex and Pearson. Pearson understood and said nothing.

Alex, being Alex, said, "Dude. You'd think we were dead or something. We were only a little dead."

I kept my arms around them both and pulled them alive. "Come on, let's get out of here."

We worked out way along the beach. The rest of my family met us at the car. Despite half the parking lot being wiped away by the tsunami, our car was still there. My family put the guns back in the truck when Lena caught sight of us first. She beamed bright and ran for me.

"Hussar! You're alive!" she called as she leaped into my arms. I caught her as she wrapped her arms around my neck. She hugged me for all she was worth, and I held my breath until she was done. She jumped from me to Alex and similarly assaulted him. "And *wujek* Alex!"

Alex smiled and blinked for a moment. He looked to me and mouthed *Wujek?*

Pearson smiled and whispered, "Uncle."

I laughed, and Alex just smiled.

Jeremy crashed into me next, turning it into a full tackle. "Dad dad dad! That was *awesome!* The dragon was like *I am a god,* and you're like *puny god,* and *blam* and you hit it with the beam from the Death Star and—"

I smiled at him. "Yeah. It was kinda awesome."

Jeremy and Lena landed at the same time. He hugged her tightly. "And you were *cool.* The sand storm and the salt storm and the *pow* with the weapons, and—"

I tuned Jeremy out as I walked towards Mariel. She smiled at me and drifted closer. "Hey."

"Hey."

We came together in an intense embrace. Our lips crashed together, and we stayed that way in the middle of the parking lot, like Bogart and Bergman. At that moment, I never wanted to be separated from my wife ever again.

After a while, Sinead coughed. And coughed again. Then she poked me with a pen. "Break it up, you two. We should get out of here before someone tries to interrogate us."

We broke it up with a smile, and we promised to resume at the next possible instance.

It was time to go back home.

GETTING HOME WAS A LITTLE DIFFICULT. MOST OF THE ROADS were flooded. The roads that weren't flooded were filled with debris. We spent most of the time going through back roads and high ground.

We got back to the summer house before actual nightfall kicked in. The cops had not shown up on our doorstep, so we were clear there. The guns were left in the car for the time being. Lena and Jeremy were the first to run out of the car and onto the porch. Sinead trailed after them since she didn't want the house burned down.

Alex and Pearson strolled out, sticking together. Alex shuffled through his deck of metal cards, telling him how the grapefruit trick worked.

Mariel stayed in the car with me, in the passenger seat. She sat with me for a long moment, holding my hand. "You okay, hon?"

I smiled at her. "More or less. It's been ... it's been a long day. The monks yesterday were horrible. Dying yesterday? Also horrible. And to be honest? I thought we were all toast. We battled Tiamat today. And we won?" I shrugged. "I can't imagine what comes next. Especially if winning looks like the devastation we drove through."

Mariel squeezed my hand. "We'll get through this, Tommy. We always do."

I looked at her with a smile. "Probably." I looked at the line of people who had trudged out into the house already. "Want to head in? I'll start cooking in a few minutes. I need some time."

She gave my hand a final squeeze, longer than the last. "Okay. If you're sure."

I flickered a smile at her. "Aren't I always?"

Mariel took a deep breath and got out of the car. I enjoyed the peace and quiet as she strode inside.

It had been a lot to process. I had guessed right when I asked for the Soul Stone from the Vatican. I hadn't even known that my ring would be drained before the big showdown. I didn't know my armor was going to be trashed to heck and back.

On the one hand, I felt ready to retire. From being an action wonder worker. From being a cop. Perhaps we could rent the summer home from Sinead during the rest of the year. Maybe even take up a hobby that didn't put all of us in danger.

On the other hand, if I hadn't done everything we had done, Tiamat would be destroying the world right now. Or would God have just sent someone else?

Then again, if I weren't minimally qualified, would I be sent out to fight the forces of Hell? Probably not.

I sighed and opened the door. The only way to move on was to move on. Tomorrow would bring its own trouble. The entire coastline was ravaged. Fires had dotted the road on the way home. Tomorrow would be a nightmare as the entire state picked up the pieces. In reality, it would turn out that half the Eastern seaboard was on fire or flooded.

And this was what victory looked like.

But that's tomorrow's problem.

I walked to the front porch and reached for the door handle.

Then the porch swing creaked.

I pivoted to the swing and reached for my gun.

There was a teenage girl, sitting in the bench. She was pretty in a vague sort of way. She had long black hair, vaguely Semitic features. She had a deep tan, a complexion that described her as Persian, perhaps Egyptian. She was definitely from somewhere in the Middle East.

Israeli? I thought. And I started to get a hint of an explanation.

She wore blue jeans and a loose-fitting white sweater. It wasn't exactly a crown of stars and a blue gown, but I suspected that she only dressed up for special occasions.

I relaxed. "My son asked me what you were like," I told her. "Should I call him out so you two can talk?"

She gave me an enigmatic little smile. "I don't think so." She patted the seat next to her. "Sit. Please. You and I should chat about a few things."

I sat. "Jeremy tells me that, usually, conversations like this come *before* all the charisms. If not with you, than with your Son."

"Would you have believed it?" she answered. She gave a tiny smile. "I wasn't consulted about it, but consider how many times you've resisted the term *wonder worker*, I can't imagine that I could have come up to you and told you who I was without proper identification."

I nodded. She was partially correct. I knew she was supernatural because she hadn't been there until I head the porch swing creak. I knew she wasn't evil because I trusted my sense of smell. I knew who she was without her telling me because Jeremy had asked the question.

"I think you have a question for me?" she prompted.

I did. I didn't even know what it was until it popped out of my mouth and I blurted, "Why me?"

She shrugged kindly. "Why not you?"

"I'm not that good."

She gave me a cynical, sardonic look that I was more familiar with from Alex. "At least acknowledge that you're good *enough* in the face of persistent, *unrelenting*, pure *evil*. You still are."

"But I have such a temper—"

Holy Mary, Mother of God, swatted me on the nose like I was a misbehaving dog who needed a warning shot. "Stop it. Your idea of a temper is centered on injustice. It's impatience with evil. It's impatience with stupidity—which some up there debate is the greatest evil. Saint Joseph and I wondered if you or Packard were going to go after Bishop Ashley.

"You'll just have to live with it. You don't ... totally stink?" she said, speaking as though the term were new to her. It may have been. She continued, "You were given everything you needed when you needed it in order to deal with the situation. You were the best man for the job. In the beginning, the demon was coming, and someone had to fight it. Someone who could withstand the wrath of the cult, and later, the warlock. Someone who could battle the Fowlers and Kozbar. Someone who could resist Jayden and her ilk. That someone happened to be you."

I sighed and nodded. She was right about all of it. I had luck. I had skills. And I always asked for the charisms I needed, not the ones I wanted.

She smiled at me. "I especially like how you keep adding *please* to prayers when you're asking for a miracle. And you don't abuse them. You only ask when you have need. How can you think this is a bad thing?"

I sighed and nodded. "You have a point."

"I know I do."

"Why did we get more help from Bokor than the bishop?"

"Because unlike the Bishop, Bokor believed in the supernatural." She rolled her eyes in annoyance at the Bishop. "Even he had a moral code, you know. Your bokor. I believe you have a saying these days—take what you want, but pay for it?"

"I've heard it."

Mary shrugged. "In the case of Baracus, it was a bit broader."

"What will happen to him?"

"That is known only to Heaven. And I haven't asked. Not my department." She giggled. "I'm more the appeals court. But to save one person is to save the whole world. In his case, he helped you save the whole world. So, you never know."

I nodded. I guess I wasn't fair to ask about the states of another man's soul. "And me? Do I have to keep doing this?"

She looked at me kindly. "Thomas, would you really be able to say no if someone asked you for help?"

"You know the answer to that."

"Yes, I do. But *you* have to acknowledge it." She patted my shoulder as she rose to her feet. "Don't worry. You have a break coming up soon."

I arched a brow and watched her walk to the edge of the porch. "What do you mean?"

"You'll know." She walked around the edge of the house and out of sight.

I didn't have to look to know that she was gone.

I stayed out on the porch for another minute, thinking over the encounter.

The front door opened. "Tommy?" Mariel asked. "You still need another minute?"

I sighed. "Nope." I rose. "I'm ready."

I walked inside with my wife. The kids were building something Lego and Star Wars on the table. Alex, Pearson and Sinead were at the dining room table, an open bottle of Jack Daniels between them. Alex poured, which was always a dangerous proposition.

It was home. Maybe not my house, but my home.

Pearson looked at me and smiled. "Detective! I just wanted to let you know that I got a message from XO. We have some additional training we'd like you to go through back in Rome. We also want you to cross-train with two other people. A Marco Catalano and an Amanda Colt. Have you heard of them? They're also from New York. Greenpoint, apparently?"

I shrugged. "I never heard of either one of them. Then again, I've spent most of my career in Eastern Queens. Should I have?"

"I'm told they're a big deal in their local circles."

I shrugged. "No idea. How about we talk about this tomorrow? I'd like to spend the rest of my time with the family."

Pearson's eyes lit up. "About that. They can come with, if you like."

"Huh." I looked to Mariel. "So, honey, what do you think about a few months in Rome?"

"Sounds like fun."

"I can't wait."

Alex poured a glass and slid it towards me. I swept it up and raised it high. "To Rome. And to God. And may God bless us, every one."

Tomorrow would be a day to help with the cleanup. We would heal the sick and bury the dead. We would dig through rubble and fight more fires.

But for now, we were home.

Did you enjoy the book?

Why not tell others about it? The best way to help an author and to spread word about books you love is to leave a review.

If you enjoyed reading DEUS VULT, can you please leave a review on Amazon for it? Good, bad, or mediocre, we want to hear from *you*. Declan and all of us at Silver Empire would greatly appreciate it.

Thank you!

ACKNOWLEDGMENTS

I'd like to start by thanking all of the usual suspects.

Gail and Margaret Konecsni of Just Write! Ink, Hans Schantz, Jim McCoy, Daniel Humphreys, Russell and Morgon Newquist, and L. Jagi Lamplighter—for all of the edits, suggestions, reviews and encouragement.

Thanks to all of the Kickstarter backers who made these awesome covers possible.

Thanks to Larry Correia's Monster Hunter International Facebook group for the gun data. Any mistakes are mine, as always.

And, as always, Vanessa.

I'd like to note that the references used over the course of this book include *The Rite* by Matt Baglio and *An Exorcist Tells His Story* by Father Amorth.

All of the prayers I use in here are real. Though some are edited and spliced together for dramatic purposes. Some include Psalms 17, 35, 54 and 63, hike! Also, the exorcism prayer of Pope Leo XIII.

What I do to Essex, Massachusetts, is fictional. Every place is fictional, even the geographic locations. If you think that you know a person/place/thing that exists in Essex, please let me know. I will pretend that I meant to do that.

While I think about it, there is a brief mention of Sri Lanka here. The experience of how the information was disseminated is real, and taken from my own experience.

ABOUT DECLAN FINN

Declan Finn lives in a part of New York City unreachable by bus or subway. Who's Who has no record of him, his family, or his education. He has been trained in hand to hand combat and weapons at the most elite schools in Long Island, and figured out nine ways to kill with a pen when he was only fifteen. He escaped a free man from Fordham University's PhD program, and has been on the run ever since. There was a brief incident where he was branded a terrorist, but only a court order can unseal those records, and really, why would you want to know?

BB bookbub.com/authors/declan-finn

f facebook.com/DeclanFinnBooks

🐦 twitter.com/DeclanFinnBooks

SILVER EMPIRE

Keep up with all the new releases, sneak peeks, appearances and more with the empire. Sign up for our Newsletter today!

Or join fellow readers in our Facebook Fan Group, the Silver Empire Legionnaires. Enjoy memes, fan discussions and more.

DEUS VULT

ST. TOMMY, NYPD BOOK SIX

By Declan Finn

Published by Silver Empire

https://silverempire.org/

This is a work of fiction. Names, characters, businesses, places, events and incidents are either the products of the author's imagination or used in a fictitious manner. Any resemblance to actual persons, living or dead, or actual events is purely coincidental.

Cover by Steve Beaulieu

CPSIA information can be obtained
at www.ICGtesting.com
Printed in the USA
BVHW031403251119
564772BV00005B/35/P